SLING SHOT
CIRCUIT RIDER

D1602206

RANDY POGUE

5 Fold Media
Visit us at www.5foldmedia.com

ENDORSEMENTS

"If you like history, if you like to hear stories of faith in action, if you like a real life hero, you will love *Sling Shot Circuit Rider* by author Randy Pogue. Randy has a unique talent of weaving historical events, real life stories, and biblical values together to produce a tapestry of life. In his new book, *Sling Shot Circuit Rider,* he does just that. As you read this book, you will find yourself riding the trails side by side with the circuit rider of a day long forgotten. This book will inform you, encourage you, and challenge you to 'ride the trail' that God has for you today."

Pastor Gary Brothers
Cape First, Cape Girardeau, MO

"As I began reading the book, I was drawn into the story line and the Travers Family. Although the characters are fictional, the historical setting is accurate. It gave me great insight into what life and ministry were like in the early 1800s—as a citizen and circuit rider. I could not put it down! The twists and turns will also draw you in. This book is an engaging read and very well written."

Pastor Ed Rhodes
Trinity United Methodist Church, Piedmont, MO

"Once I started reading *Sling Shot Circuit Rider,* I couldn't put it down. I love the way Randy weaves fiction and history together. As a pastor, I was entertained, challenged, and convicted all at the same time. I had no idea that the circuit-riding preachers played such an important role in the taming of the American West. I congratulate Brother Pogue on his excellent research, creativity, and writing skills. I hope that this book finds its way into many homes and hearts, and blesses them the way that it has me."

Dr. Steve Proctor
Pastor of Westwood Baptist Church, Poplar Bluff, MO

Acknowledgments

Proverbs 18:22 tells us that "Whoso findeth a wife findeth a good thing, and obtaineth favour of the Lord." Few things in my life have brought me as much joy and a sense of goodness as the wife I have found. Along with my three beautiful children, I truly feel favored of the Lord and give Him thanks continually for my family. A huge thank you goes out to my wife, Missy, for her invaluable suggestions and occasional criticisms of the early drafts of this book; both of which added immeasurably to the development of the writing and the writer.

I would also like to express my sincere appreciation and love for my dear mother, Flossie Pogue, as well as my in-laws, Mel and Barb Rowland, for their continual support and encouragement with this book, but most of all in my weekly ministry.

A debt of gratitude is due to Mary Jane Franklin and Carol Knollhoff for their tireless effort and interest in the preliminary editing of my book. These dear ladies, from the Arcadia Valley Assembly of God church, have truly gone above and beyond the call of duty – and their labor of love has not gone unnoticed or unappreciated.

Many thanks to a "world changer," Brandon Warren, for the four great illustrations he created for this book.

Finally, a big thank you goes out to the folks at 5 Fold Media for helping me realize a dream. Thank you for your patience and professionalism during this journey together.

DEDICATION

This book is dedicated to my late father, Dallas Pogue,
who was a great admirer of the American western novel,
but more importantly, a great lover of the Lord.

CONTENTS

FOREWORD

Sling Shot Circuit Rider is a captivating and historical account of early settlers in areas of southeastern Missouri from a religious perspective. The scope of this book depicts the influence of Christianity on our nation's foundation by following the life and experience of a young circuit riding minister.

Indeed, in reading this book you are able to experience the realities of settling the American frontier. The characters in the story reflect tragedies, celebrations, conflict, romance, and the miraculous transformation of lives changed by the Word of God. Even though considered by many in those days as unimportant, mission work among the Native Americans was part of the expansion of the gospel in the wilderness.

Although told with fictional main characters, the rest of the characters, the places, and the historical and geographical events are real. This setting provides the reader with a sense of witnessing the formation of early settlements of the state of Missouri. The book is a good read and a very inspiring work.

James G. McHaffie, Director of Missions
Southern Missouri District of the Assemblies of God

INTRODUCTION

How was the West won? Ever since I was a young boy I have been intrigued by tales of conquering the untamed American West and the resulting advancement of civilization and progress. But what elements played integral roles in this "winning of the West?" I have read and understood the impact that rivers and railroads made in allowing fortune-seekers and families alike to filter westward. I have also enjoyed stories of outlaws and Indian attacks with the slow but steady influx of law and order as corruptness gave way to civilization and society formed out of savagery. Yet, there is one element that is all too often neglected when considering the formative years of this great nation. The element of which I speak is the influence of religious faith, not just any faith but Christian faith.

Of immeasurable impact was the influence of both the First and Second Great Awakenings, which were national revivals impacting both the late 18th and early 19th centuries. Not only was there a notable increase in the number of Americans professing faith in Christ, but the Bible (already recognized as an influential book), was increasingly touted as the standard for morality and truth in this melting pot of humanity's "huddled masses yearning to breathe free." It is further evidenced from the inscriptions on monuments scattered throughout our land, as well as the revolutionary documents on which our nation was founded.

But it was not only our founders who were influenced by these early revivals; perhaps the greatest impact lay in the common people spreading across the vast expanse of the American West. The camp meetings in the early 1800s—along with the itinerant revivalists—offered a grassroots, non-traditional Christianity that appealed to the people pouring into these uncharted regions. The Methodist circuit-riding preacher was just one component of this formative influence. Along with the Baptists, the

Methodists were among the fastest growing churches influencing the young country after the Revolutionary War period. It has been reported that in 1775 fewer than one out of every eight hundred Americans were Methodists. By 1812, however, the statistic had changed to one out of every thirty-six Americans being a Methodist. The itinerant preacher was a key component to this success, for it was he who traveled the long, lonely roads to the many remote villages and scattered farms. In 1795, ninety-five percent of Americans lived in places with fewer than 2,500 inhabitants with little fluctuation in that statistic over the next thirty years.[1] The circuit-riding preacher offered the life-changing message of the gospel, encouragement, and leadership to many who would not otherwise have been able to attract or afford a minister. This all too often neglected component of the "winning of the West" most assuredly helped pave the way for the strong republic in which we are blessed to live today.

It is for this reason that I chose to write this book. My hope and prayer is that this fictional story—built upon actual historical people, places, and events—will not only inform the reader of our rich, religious heritage, but will perhaps inspire us as well to exhibit an increased commitment in our service to the Almighty. For the reality is that there are still many who have not yet received an adequate presentation of the gospel message that Jesus died on the cross for the forgiveness of our sins and rose again the third day that we may have hope of eternal life with Him.

---

1. John H. Wigger, "Holy, 'Knock-'Em-Down' Preachers," *Christian History Magazine*, #45, 22.

CHAPTER 1
INDIAN ATTACK

Louisiana Territory, Fall 1803

It was early fall and the trees along Castor River were beginning to scatter the forest floor with new shades of yellow and orange. A young buck stood at a bend in the creek enjoying a drink before coming to alert at the sound of approaching footsteps. Lost in his thoughts, the walking man failed to notice the startled buck; neither did he take time to enjoy the colorful scenery along the beaten path from the mines to his cabin. The La Motte mine had been buzzing with talk of Indian attacks up and down the Great River over the last few days.[2] A traveler from Sainte Genevieve brought the latest news that very morning and the foreboding atmosphere was such that management had given permission to men with families to leave early to protect their loved ones in case of an Indian attack. The word was that a band of Creek Indians, especially embittered over the ever-increasing white population and already prone to excessively aggressive behavior, had been expelled from their tribes on account of crimes and had gone about killing and burning houses.

Harrison's thoughts were racing as he thought of Vera and the kids. Preparations had to be made. He would need to bring extra wood into the house and pen the animals in the barn. *Filthy Indians*, he thought as his mind went back to his first encounter with Indians since coming to the Upper Louisiana Territory a couple of years back. He had run into a small band of Osage Indians while hunting one very cold day in the latter part of the fall of 1801. The Osage were tall, over six feet, armed with

---

2 Historical Note: The Mississippi River was often times referred to as the "Great River" in this time period.

bows and arrows as they were obviously hunting for their winter meat. Although the Osage villages were several miles further west, he had been told the Osage still considered everything east to the Great River their hunting grounds.

Over the last couple of days he had traveled some twenty miles west of his cabin on Castor River to a beautiful valley another miner had spoken of where the game was plentiful and it was "just plain somethin' to see," the miner had exclaimed. He had his mules, Zeke and Jeb, along and had killed a nice buck that morning. He was in the process of loading it onto Zeke when the band of Indians had appeared, seemingly out of nowhere. Bows drawn and faces hard, the band of six warriors closed in around him. One broad shouldered brave, with a deep scar on his left cheek, grabbed the lead ropes for the mules.

An older warrior with a scowling gaze came as close as two feet of him and spoke forcefully in French, "Qu'est-ce que vous faites ici? Cette terre appartient à nous!" Harrison, born an Englishman and having only spent a couple years with some French in the Sainte Genevieve area, was weak in his French communication. Yet, it was not hard to figure out that they were not pleased to find him there and with game. He caught the word *terre*, which means "land," so in his limited French he boldly replied "Partagez la terre" (share the land). The older warrior struck him across the face, which he took standing—facing the Indian with firm resolve. Whooping and hollering, each Indian in turn struck Harrison, making their exit with his mules, deer, and gun! Knocked from his feet with the sudden and forceful blows, Harrison cursed the Indians through bloody lips.

The twenty mile walk back to his cabin on Castor River was the most difficult trek of his life. The frigid temperature, along with at least a couple of broken ribs and one arm badly cut from a knife blade from the scar-faced Indian, took its toll on his body as he struggled homeward. "Revenge," he vowed, "I'll make the filthy Indians pay!"

His thoughts returned to Vera and the children alone at home. He must hurry, must get ready in case the Creek Indians make it this far west of the Great River.

A sudden gunshot invaded his thoughts, reverberating through the crisp October air and sending a chill up his spine. "Vera!" he yelled as he splashed across the river, running at full speed the last quarter mile to the cabin. As he drew closer he could hear a few whoops and the bellow of another gun shot. His only weapon was a pistol in his waistband that he kept with him on his trips back and forth to the mines—protection against the unknown. He left his black-powder rifle with Vera and the kids.

Jed was twelve years old now and able to help Harrison with bringing home some meat. It was not uncommon for Jed to meet Harrison some evenings coming home from the mines with a couple squirrels or a rabbit held high in his hand. "Look dad! Got us some vittles for supper," Jed would say with a big smile across his face.

It was his own black-powder rifle that he heard a third time as he broke through the oak grove just west of his cabin. An Indian lay sprawled on the ground not fifty yards from the front of the cabin. Pistol in hand, he ran to the cabin yelling for his wife. Laura, his ten-year-old daughter, met him at the door with tears streaming down her face. Vera, putting another load in the rifle, peered out the back window of the cabin. "They've gone," she stated flatly and then with a moan said, "Jed was fetchin' water when they came…I haven't seen him."

Harrison took the rifle and went back out the door, taking a careful look before rounding the corner of the cabin towards the well. The barn was on fire and it looked like his gray mare was gone. That would have to wait. Where was Jed?

Convinced that the Indians had left, he sprinted toward the well, Vera and Laura following closely behind. A growing fear gripped his stomach. *If they hurt that boy...* He stopped suddenly; Jed lay five feet from the well with two arrows protruding from his back.

Vera screamed and ran to the lifeless body, falling on him in anguish. Laura stood over Vera with her face in her hands, sobbing uncontrollably. Harrison's heart felt like it had broken in two.

Suddenly, anger boiled up inside of him. "I'll kill 'em…I'll kill 'em all!" he screamed.

CHAPTER 2
UNEXPECTED FRIENDS

Logan County, KY, 1798

Ten-year-old William Travers stood perfectly still with his sling held at the ready. The grey squirrel William had spotted moments before was making its way down the oak tree, unaware of the impending danger. *Just a few more feet*, he thought to himself as the squirrel paused on a limb to survey its surroundings. His heart was pounding with excitement as he waited for the squirrel to get into range. Given that he had been practicing for weeks with stones from along the banks of the Gaspar River, he had become quite accurate with targets up to thirty steps. The added challenge, however, was that the necessary motion of swinging the sling often alerted the prey at that critical moment before the stone was launched, thus creating a moving target. If, by chance, he could launch the stone with the animal's attention held elsewhere he could overcome this obstacle. Wouldn't Pa be so proud if he came back with a squirrel harvested from a sling made with his own hands! He had made several attempts that morning, but each one had failed. With each experience, however, he gained valuable knowledge and he simply would not accept defeat.

Partially hidden behind a tree and some shrub brush he stood perfectly still as the squirrel scurried down the tree and across a fallen log towards him. The unsuspecting critter then began scratching in the leaves within twenty-five steps of him.

Letting out a slow breath, he took careful aim and let the stone fly. The startled squirrel jumped and quickly scurried back up the oak, seemingly unharmed. In exasperation, William threw down the sling and kicked it several feet for good measure. It was then he heard a muffled laugh

16

from behind him. He turned quickly, fear gripping him as he saw a young Indian boy standing not thirty feet away from him.

William stood transfixed; his breath seemed to have escaped him. Were there others close by ready to capture or kill him? Suddenly the young Indian, slightly larger than William and carrying a bow and quiver of arrows across his shoulder, began walking toward him, still laughing softly to himself. William's feet wouldn't seem to move; he simply stood, staring dumbly at the approaching stranger.

The Indian boy walked past William and bent over to pick up the sling. He turned it in his hands, inspecting it closely. He then picked up a small stone from the ground, placed it in the leather strap, and swung it awkwardly. He let the stone fly and watched as it flew wildly into a clump of brush at the side. This strange contraption, the likes of which he had obviously never seen before, brought on another round of laughter.

Finally William found his voice and stated softly, "let me show you how to do it," as he cautiously reached for the sling. The Indian boy did not resist as William took the sling then reached in his pocket for a smooth stone.

William took careful aim at a rock, roughly six inches tall and a foot across, protruding out of the ground just under twenty feet away. The stone hit the target nearly dead center and ricocheted off with a crack.

The young Indian grunted with approval, nodding his head. William handed the sling back to the boy and took another smooth stone out of his pocket and offered it to him.

The Indian boy grasped the sling and stone and smiled widely as he again prepared for a shot. Taking careful aim at the same protruding rock, the stone hit about a foot left of the rock and shot across the leaves into a dry creek bed. He let out a whoop that startled William at first, but then the two boys looked at each other and laughed simultaneously. An instant connection formed between the two boys and they spent the afternoon using the sling as well as shooting the Indian's bow and arrow.

Suddenly, the young Indian boy motioned for William to follow him. William hesitated, not because he didn't trust his new friend, but because the day was drawing to a close and his pa and ma would be expecting him back to the cabin before supper. However, his new friend would not be deterred and took William by the hand, leading him through the woods.

Soon they entered a small clearing where three other Indians sat around a small fire. William stopped suddenly, but the Indian boy motioned for him to enter the camp.

The Indian man, who William supposed to be the father, stood and watched the two approach the fire. The boy and his father spoke briefly in a language that William could not understand, then to his great surprise, the father said, "Please sit down." The Indian man noticed the shock on William's face and laughed softly before confessing, "I learned a little of your talk from white religious man across river to the north. What is your name?" he asked, motioning again for William to take a seat by the fire.

"William Travers," he answered quietly.

"Komoka say you have good weapon," began the Indian. "May I see?"

William pulled the sling from his back pocket and handed it to the man. "Is that his name, Ko…mo…ko?" he asked as he looked over at his young Indian friend.

Komoka smiled at the attempted pronunciation of his name and stated loudly and clearly, "Komoka!"

"Komoka," repeated William and smiled back.

"William," replied Komoka. The two boys chuckled as Komoka's father examined the sling.

"Can you show me how it shoot?" he asked.

William, enjoying the attention, took another smooth stone from his pocket. Taking the sling, he looked around for a good target. Spotting a small protruding rock about fifteen steps away, he stood and rotated the sling slowly twice before making an overhand throw. The stone smacked the rock and Komoka let out another whoop which immediately brought laughter from his father.

"Good shot," he exclaimed as he once again took the sling to examine it.

William glanced over at the two women who were sitting quietly by the fire. He assumed they were Komoka's mother and older sister; the older woman looked very weak and frail.

Komoka's father observed William's gaze and explained that they had been separated from their traveling party some days back due to an illness that had fallen upon his wife. A large number of Delaware Indians had accepted an invitation from the Spanish to settle in what is called the Upper Louisiana Territory, which is just across the Great River to the west. When his wife had regained her strength they would join their family and tribe near an area that was called New Madrid.

William felt a bit of pride well up in him knowing that he was in an Indian camp and being treated with respect, although just a boy. *What will Pa think of all this*? he thought to himself, as a gripping twinge of dread came over him, realizing he should be home by now. He graciously excused himself and explained his need to get home, but before he could turn to go, Komoka took his hand and placed within it an amulet of some sort. It had a claw of a bear, a tooth of another animal that he was unsure of, and a small feather all attached to a rawhide strap.

Komoka spoke something to William which he couldn't understand, but his father explained that this was very special to his son. The amulet had been a gift from his grandfather many moons back and was given to him before his first hunt. Komoka believed that it gave him good luck while on the hunt. Perhaps it would bring good luck to his new friend as well.

William felt like he could cry, but he dared not show tears to his new friends. His heart swelled with such appreciation that he couldn't speak for a long moment. Finally, with a cracking voice he managed to murmur a simple thank you. He remembered something his pa had said—Indians very much like to trade. A grin formed on his lips as he handed his sling to Komoka. Komoka's eyes beamed with joy as he accepted the gift. Once again, Komoka let out a whoop and everyone broke into laughter. William took one last glimpse back at his new friend before heading back into the woods, wondering if he would ever see Komoka again.

CHAPTER 3
RIGHT CHOICES?

Travers' Cabin on Gaspar River

Where is that boy, mused Jacob as he sat on a homemade chair skinning a couple of squirrels he had killed a few hours before with his rifle. The sun would be setting within the hour and William had his chores to finish up before supper. *Probably out exploring again*, he considered as he finished up the last squirrel and propped his feet up on a small table, enjoying the view of the sun glistening off of the river.

"Not many young-uns for the boy to play with out here," he said out loud to himself as he studied. Had he been too rash in his decision to move his family out here? They had a nice home back in North Carolina and his business had been good, making and repairing shoes. Sarah had misgivings about moving to the new territory in Kentucky but was willing; the loss of their seven-year-old daughter to whooping cough a few summers back probably had as much to do with her agreeing to leave as anything else. Everything around Sarah sparked memories of Susan, and she was wilting—they all were. Nothing had quite prepared them, however, for the challenges they would face out here. Sure, he had caught the passion of wanting to see the West. Like so many others back East, he had felt that beast rising up in him to see untamed territory, interact with the Indians, live off the land, and explore the unknown. Western Kentucky provided all of that but there were challenges that he had not fully understood—the loneliness most of all. It wasn't that big of a deal to him really, but Sarah longed for other womenfolk to visit with and to take part in church socials and the like. Their nearest neighbor was three miles away and each family spent so much time providing for their own needs that there wasn't a lot of time to go a callin'. They saw the Hansens once a month or so to trade them a couple of chickens for some bacon, but they weren't overly friendly and spoke little English so the visits weren't what you'd call pleasurable. Mostly, he worried about his boys, William and John. Was it right for him to take them away from their grandparents and their schoolin'?

"William loves the hunting and fishing and is taking to the farming, but am I limiting his potential by taking him away from the many opportunities back East?" he reflected audibly as Sarah stepped out of the cabin door.

"Are you talking to yourself again Jacob?" Sarah asked, smiling as she placed her hand on his shoulder.

"Was I wrong in bringing you and the boys out here…is this just a selfish, childish dream?" he whispered, placing his hand on hers.

Sarah walked around in front of Jacob, placing her other hand on his chin and lifting his face to look at hers. "Jacob, you are a good man, a wonderful father and husband. We are together and that is all that matters. The boys and I are doing fine and we're going to keep doing fine."

"Pa, Pa!" John yelled as he came running from the cabin with the wooden toy horse Jacob handmade for him that last Christmas in North Carolina. Sarah just laughed as John ran and jumped on Jacob's back, effectively quenching their tender moment.

"Where's Will?" John grunted as he began wrestling Jacob's neck.

"That's a good question, son," replied Jacob as he twirled John around, pinning him to the ground with a good dose of tickling.

"Speak of the devil," Sarah blurted out as her hands came to her hips in typical scolding fashion as she saw William running toward them.

"Ma, Pa, I'm so sorry that I'm late, but you're not going to believe what happened to me!" William exclaimed excitedly as he ran to the cabin, bending over to catch his breath.

"There had better be a good reason young man. Those animals have been frettin' something fierce with you making 'em wait so long for their supper," Sarah stated flatly.

"Where's that squirrel you've been promising; the one who's going to have a knot on his head by a sling and stone?" Jacob asked with a smile as he reached out to pick at the boy.

Noticing that William's back pocket was empty, Jacob asked, "Where in the world is your sling? I can't remember the last time I've seen you without it!"

"Would you believe that it's in the hands of an Indian?" William replied, taking note of the shocked expression on their faces that he had anticipated. "And he swapped me this," he continued as he pulled out the amulet Komoka had given him, displaying it with pride.

CHAPTER 4
VISITING PREACHER

A Few Weeks Later, Travers' Cabin

It was a cool morning—one of the first in many weeks as summer was about to give way to fall. William was feeding the chickens and trying to keep that rotten rooster from flogging him again when he heard the dog barking.

"I'll deal with you later," he growled at the strutting cock, giving it a good kick as he closed the chicken coop door. Heading back to the house with a half dozen eggs in a basket and thoughts of kicking a certain rooster, he saw the source of their dog's alarm riding up to the cabin on a large bay horse.

Jacob stepped out of the cabin to meet the stranger as the rider pulled his horse up to a stop and removed his hat. "Quiet Jake," Jacob scolded the dog before turning his attention to this rare sight at the Travers' homestead. "Welcome stranger, you're the first visitor we've had in probably three months I guess," Jacob declared with a warm smile. William walked up and stood next to his pa, trying to get Jake to sit down beside him and behave.

"Good morning to you folks. My name is James McGready. I'm a Presbyterian minister, just recently arrived from back East. I've taken charge of three churches in Logan County and have been traveling around inviting folks to join us for worship."

Pa's grin widened as he extended his hand to take the Reverend's. "I've got a right pretty lady in this here cabin who will be wanting to meet you," Pa chuckled. "Get yourself down and join us for some fresh eggs if you're a mind to," Jacob continued.

Mr. McGready dismounted and turned to William, "Looks like they are mighty fresh," he exclaimed looking at the basket in William's hand. "And what might your name be?" he asked as he extended a hand to William.

"My name is William, sir…William Travers."

"It is a very fine pleasure to meet you Mr. William Travers," Mr. McGready bellowed with a laugh and a broad smile that pleased William immensely.

I like Reverend James McGready, he thought to himself as they walked into the cabin together.

William's excitement wouldn't allow him to wait for Pa to make the formal introduction. "Ma, Ma," he nearly yelled as he rushed over to Sarah. "We got us a preacher a callin'! This here is Reverend James McGready."

Sarah was helping John dress, but instantly stood and briefly primped herself before extending a jubilant hand to that of Mr. McGready. "Mr. McGready, I'm Sarah Travers, and I can't begin to tell you how glad I am to meet you!"

Mr. McGready let out another one of those bellowing laughs as he shook Sarah's hand.

"It has been a spell since we have had a good dose of religion, and my soul has been aching to take Communion," Sarah continued, still holding Reverend McGready's hand. "Please take a seat, and I'll fry us up some eggs."

Mr. McGready sat down next to William at the table and began to tell the Travers family about the churches at Gaspar River, Red River, and Muddy River that he had been ministering in for a few months now. Jacob was interested to hear about Reverend McGready's time in North Carolina before coming West. Reverend McGready had even heard of Jacob's fine shoes that he had made and sold in Fayetteville. Sarah wanted to learn about Reverend McGready's parents who, as it turns out, were Scotch Irish Presbyterians from Pennsylvania. She was fascinated by how he was called to preach, and about his ministry travels and experiences. William soaked it all in; he seldom had the chance to learn about so many places and to hear such good stories. Reverend McGready had a booming voice and spoke with a strong passion about God. William couldn't wait to go to the Gaspar River church the next Sunday and hear Reverend McGready again.

CHAPTER 5
GASPAR RIVER CHURCH

Logan County, KY, Spring 1800

The last two years had gone by quickly for William and his family. More and more families were moving into Logan County and Jacob had found a market for his shoes again. William, being the oldest son and adept at working with his hands, had been learning his father's trade. Every three weeks or so the family had been attending the Gaspar River church where the Reverend James McGready consistently brought forth a fiery message. Sarah had reveled in the Sunday afternoon dinner on the grounds and had made several new friends among those who had been moving into the county. Although the Gaspar River congregation was small, there seemed to be a hunger growing for more of God.

Sarah, having been raised in a Presbyterian home back in North Carolina, quickly committed herself to the church and became involved with fasting and prayer for the conversion of sinners in Logan County. This fasting was established on the third Saturday of each month for all of his congregations. William had been in awe of the powerful messages that came forth from Reverend McGready. When the good reverend would talk about heaven, it was as if William could envision the streets of gold and see Saint Peter himself. Equally compelling was feeling the heat from the flames when Reverend McGready talked about the eternal punishment awaiting those who rejected the Savior.

One Sunday morning in the spring of 1799 William listened intently as his pastor spoke about the sin that separates mankind from God but how Jesus had died on the cross so that a person might be forgiven. William sensed the weight of his sin and stepped forward when Reverend

26

McGready asked if there was anyone who wanted to accept Christ as their Savior. William felt as if the weight had been lifted off of him and he experienced such joy in his heart as he lifted his hands in thanks to God.

Although Jacob had faithfully taken his family to the services at the Gaspar River church and seemed to thoroughly enjoy the fellowship with the other men, he seemed reluctant to fully engage in the new-found faith of his son. Sarah got into the habit of reading the family Bible and praying with the boys each morning, but Jacob always seemed to find some chore to do outside when she pulled out the Word.

"There's to be a grand Communion service at the Red River meeting house the first weekend in June," declared Reverend McGready one Sunday morning. "We'll be inviting the Methodists, Baptists, and all who will come!" He continued. "Services will begin on Friday and finish up on Monday. Be sure and bring provisions for the whole time if you can manage it at all, but of course you're welcome to come for a night or two if that's all you can manage."

The Red River church was some fifteen miles or so southwest of the Gaspar River church. The distance, however, seemed irrelevant as the congregation began making plans to attend. The anticipation was almost palpable. For several months the spirit of revival was in the air as a number of folks throughout the county had been touched by the Lord. Great things were expected from what many would later call their first "camp meeting."

Sarah was elated as they loaded the family in the wagon and headed for home. "Can you imagine it Jacob…maybe hundreds of people coming together from all walks of faith to worship the Lord?"

"And we get to camp out for four days," William piped in, clearly sharing his mother's enthusiasm.

John began fidgeting with his dress tie, anxious to rid himself of the itchy nuisance.

"What about our animals?" Jacob mused.

"Surely we can come up with something; maybe Mr. Hansen's son would be willing to come over each day to feed them," replied Sarah, plainly determined not to let anything sour her enthusiasm.

It's obvious that Ma had set her mind on this issue, Jacob thought as the corners of his mouth turned up slightly. He had to admit that his curiosity was piqued. "It does sound exciting," he admitted.

"Can we bring Jake along?" William pleaded, his head bobbing up and down between Jacob and Sarah as they rode along.

"Jake, Jake!" John piped in with excitement.

"Now that would get folks jumping in the spirit with Jake chasing a rabbit or squirrel across their laps in the meeting house," Sarah said with a laugh.

"Jake, Jake is coming to church!" yelled John as everyone laughed at the mental picture of Jake raising the roof.

CHAPTER 6
RED RIVER COMMUNION SERVICE

Logan County, KY, June 1800

There was great excitement in the air as the wagons began pouring in for the highly anticipated four-day event. It was quite amazing how word could spread so quickly across the hills and hollows of this wild country. There were folks who had ridden close to one hundred miles just to see what the Lord might do. And just like Reverend McGready had said, there seemed to be folks from all walks of faith and life—Methodists, Baptists, whites, blacks, poor farmers, and well-to-do townspeople.

The Travers family made camp next to a family from the Muddy River congregation who had a boy about William's age. The two hit it off immediately, and as soon as they had helped their parents set up camp they were off exploring. William had made another sling at which he had grown quite adept over the last couple of years. He took great pride in impressing his new-found friend with his marksmanship. But what most impressed his friend was the Indian amulet that Komoka had given him.

Friday, Saturday, and Sunday passed quietly with lots of singing and plenty of good food and hospitality with local ministers taking turns bringing a message. Sarah commented that this may be a little taste of what heaven will be like with people from all walks of life eating together and sharing freely. William was thoroughly enjoying himself; playing with his new friend, meeting many new people, and hearing the Word of God brought forth in many different ways and styles.

The family from the Muddy River congregation camping next to the Travers was very musical and participated considerably in the worship times during the meetings. Peter, William's new young friend, was learning to play the fiddle from his pa. Peter and his father played fiddles while Peter's ma and sister sang.

"That girl can sing like an angel," Sarah exclaimed one evening after the meeting.

William had to agree, he thought she looked quite like an angel as well. At least he figured an angel couldn't be much prettier than she was.

A rotund lady from the Red River congregation, who obviously regarded herself as quite the singer, sang every evening. "That there lady would give ol' Jake a reason to howl now wouldn't she?" Jacob said one morning during breakfast.

"She reminds me of two pigs a fighting," he exclaimed. Jacob's comment drew a lot of laughs from William, Peter, and his pa, but a quick slap on the arm from Sarah.

On Monday something utterly fantastic occurred during the service. As one local minister preached, a woman started shouting and singing. Several in the meeting began to weep and cry out to God. An overwhelming sense of God's presence seemed to fill the whole place, causing many to seek the Lord for assurance of salvation. At the onset, William was caught up watching different folks around him as they were shouting and crying. Suddenly, he felt the power of God strong upon him as he lifted his hands and began praising the Lord with all of his might. At that moment, he became unconcerned about what others might think or say. His only desire was to fully surrender himself to the Lord. His awareness of everyone around him slipped away and it was just he and Jesus. An overwhelming sense of God's love—not only for himself but for the world—came over William. He immediately began crying out over and over, "Use me Lord to show people your love...use me Jesus."

In that moment, William experienced something that he would never forget and that would influence the rest of his life. An image appeared in his mind of this vast new country that he and his family called home—a wild country full of people in need of God's love. He then saw himself among many other saints of God spreading west across this vast land teaching the Word of God to whites, blacks, Indians, and everyone who would receive the good news of the gospel.

Chapter 7
A Transformed Father

The Travers' Homestead, 1800

News of the happenings at the Red River meeting house spread like wildfire. Plans were already underway to have another meeting at the Gaspar River church in July. Although Jacob had seemed to enjoy himself at the event, he had seemed withdrawn and sullen since the family's return to their home on the Gaspar River.

Sarah, concerned and sleepless one night in late June, told her husband, "Jacob, we can never bring up the children proper without family prayer."

"I know you're right Sarah," Jacob replied quietly, "but I...I simply don't know how to pray." With Sarah's encouragement, Jacob was finally convinced to trade off with her in leading prayer with the boys each day.

The next morning, Sarah led the prayer after reading a Psalm out of the family Bible. The following day Jacob seemed very nervous, but willing nonetheless, to read a passage out of the Gospels that Sarah had selected. When it came time for Jacob to lead in family prayer, it was as if God had sought him out. Jacob fell to his knees, trembling slightly, and began to cry out to God. It was as if a tremendous sense of guilt and helplessness had struck him and he began to confess his selfishness and pride to the Lord.

Sarah and William prayed and cried as they watched their Savior do a mighty work in Jacob. William had never been so proud of his dad than at that moment.

Although Jacob had always been a wonderful father, the next few weeks were a tremendous testimony to William of what the Holy Spirit can do. Jacob, a transformed man and father, was now eager to read the Bible both on his own and with the family. And although he had always been loving towards William and John, there now seemed to be a tenderness in Jacob that William had never seen in his father before.

31

Chapter 8
Uncle Zeb

Gaspar River, August 1801

Communicating with family back east was not an easy task but the mail system in western Kentucky, although slow, was making great strides in improving efficiency and speed. Sarah attempted to write to her family back in North Carolina every couple months and when a return letter arrived it was always a big family event at the Travers' home. Sarah's sister Martha not only kept them updated on her family's affairs but she also kept in touch with some of Jacob's family.

One day, Jacob had just returned home with some supplies and his yell brought the family running, "Mail, mail…we've got mail!"

William had been practicing with his sling out behind the house while John was playing with Jake. Both boys began racing to see who could get to Pa first with Jake nippin' at their heels.

Sarah, washing some clothes down by the river, dropped everything and came running to meet Jacob.

"Let me put the horse up while you get me something to eat, then we can see what the folks back East have to say," Jacob stated as he held out the letter to Sarah. Sarah began pulling on the letter which held fast between Jacob's whitening fingers.

"You give me that letter Jacob Travers or you'll be cookin' your own meals the rest of the week," she replied, hitting Jacob on the leg.

Jacob laughed as he released the letter and dismounted. Searching out a cool spot under a shade tree, Sarah opened the letter, the boys gathering in close around her.

"I didn't figure I would get anything to eat; I should have hid that letter in my britches until after supper," Jacob continued with a big smile on his face.

Sarah just threw him a quick glance and shaking her head went right back to the letter. As she read through the letter her head would bob, interrupted occasionally with a sigh or a "Well, I'll be."

"Jacob, it says here that your brother, Zeb, is planning on being in Kentucky this very month and is coming to visit," Sarah said as she laid the letter in her lap. "Zeb spent several years up in the northeast didn't he?" Sarah asked.

"Yeah, he was gonna attend a school up there but I haven't heard from him in several years. Surely he's not coming out here just to see us," Jacob mused.

"This letter is dated July sixteenth, so he could actually be here any day now," Sarah concluded.

It was one week to the day when Zeb came riding in on a buckskin with a loaded-down pack mule in tow. William hadn't seen his Uncle Zeb for probably six years but he would never forget that nose. Uncle Zeb was always one for wrestling and Jacob had told him and John about the night that his uncle had a big wrestling match with a mean German lad back in Fayetteville. As Pa tells it, that lad got so angry when Zeb pinned him that he reached up and bit a big chunk out of Zeb's nose. All William remembered was that he couldn't keep his eyes off of Zeb's nose any time he was around, it fascinated him because it was so funny looking.

Zeb was the first kin to visit the family since their leaving North Carolina, and that made this an extra special day. Sarah killed one of the hens to fry up for supper while Jacob and the boys showed Zeb around the place.

"What brings you out this way, Zeb? Surely you didn't travel all this way just to visit us?" Jacob asked.

"Actually I've been over at Cane Ridge, about twenty miles west of Lexington. Ma told me that you all had settled on the Gaspar River so I couldn't pass up the chance to come a little farther west and see you and the family," Zeb said as he put William in a head lock.

"Have you been doing any wrestling boy?" Zeb asked William as he proceeded to put William in a hold that nearly cut off his wind.

"I'll have to give you some pointers while I'm here," Zeb said, finally releasing William and rubbing his head playfully. William's excitement clearly expressed his answer.

"You don't mean to tell me that you came all the way from New Jersey on horseback to attend that big "Communion" they scheduled over there this month?" Jacob asked.

"Well yes, actually that is one reason for my trip," Zeb explained. "You see, I'm peddling books and publications, as well as doing a little bit of writing myself. A lot of folks back East are curious about these religious happenings here in western Kentucky and I thought I might experience some of it and write about it. There are several newspapers and the like who pay pretty well for the happenings out West," he continued. "I've found a lot of folks eager to buy reading material out here as well, so I was considering exploring these parts a mite."

It wasn't long before everyone was enjoying fried chicken as they caught up on each other's adventures over the last six years. Zeb was excited to hear that Reverend James McGready lived nearby and looked forward to interviewing someone who had played an instrumental part in the revivals that were occurring across the state. Sarah enjoyed hearing about what women were wearing in New York and Philadelphia, while Jacob was interested to hear news about the young government.

Zeb had met some interesting people in his travels and he wasn't shy about bragging about it. "That Benjamin Rush is one smart fellow!" Zeb said excitably as he reached for another slice of corn bread. "He has studied medicine in Paris and London, and of course you know he was one of the signers of the Declaration of Independence. I heard him speak at a college graduation a few months back and let me tell you the man is brilliant. He's becoming a strong proponent of public education. As a matter of fact, he advocated that the US government require public schools to teach students using the Bible as a textbook and that the government furnish a Bible to every family!" Zeb continued. "That has fostered more than a little heated discussion. Undoubtedly, the Bible is by far my biggest seller," Zeb stated as he pulled a book out of one of his packs. "This here is a copy of the first English language Bible printed in the U.S., Robert

Aitken's 1782 printing of the King James Version Bible. It was illegal to print the King James Bible here before the Revolution of course."

William's eyes were fixed on the beautifully bound book and his interest did not go unnoticed. "Here boy, this here copy is a gift to you from your ol' Uncle Zeb." William held the Bible as if it were a precious jewel.

Zeb, Jacob, and Sarah talked well into the night and, for once, William was allowed to stay up past his bedtime to listen in. The most fascinating stories were those Uncle Zeb shared from his recent visit to Cane Ridge. William had heard Pastor McGready speak of plans for an even larger Communion service there. A Presbyterian pastor from Cane Ridge had traveled to witness the revivals taking place in and around Logan County and had returned with a strong desire to pass along what he had experienced with his parishioners. This pastor, by the name of Stone, had planned a Communion at Cane Ridge the first weekend in August. Uncle Zeb, who said he didn't really "buy into all this religious stuff," still seemed quite enthralled by the whole event.

"There must have been upwards of twenty thousand people swirling about the grounds watching, praying, weeping, groaning, and falling," Zeb exclaimed. "I've never seen anything quite like it. I talked to several folks throughout the event and many were convinced it was another Pentecost—a real move of God. Others believed it was a bunch of emotional hogwash and folks taking advantage of it for financial gain."

William had tried to process some of the things he had seen and heard at some of the services at the Gaspar River church over the last year or so. He was convinced that what he had experienced in his heart was real for it had never truly left him. More specifically, he knew without a doubt that Jesus now lived in his heart. What bothered him was to see some folks fall down and act all spiritual but the very next day be cussing up a storm. Listening to his ma and pa talk with Uncle Zeb about their faith made him proud.

"It's true that when people's emotions get involved that excess can occur," Sarah confirmed. "But for many, the Lord has truly touched them and you can see the change in their lives afterward," she continued passionately.

"One of the preachers explained it very well." Jacob added. "It is not how high you jump but how straight you walk when you hit the ground. For us, Zeb, Jesus is more than a revival meeting; He has truly become our everything," Jacob concluded.

Amazement spread across Zeb's face as he responded, "Little brother, that is the last thing I ever expected to hear come out of your mouth! Hey, that is great for you all, and I'm happy for you, but I'm gonna have to chew on this a little more," Zeb sighed.

Uncle Zeb journeyed a couple months around central and western Kentucky interviewing people and selling books, stopping at the Travers' cabin every chance he got. True to his word, he taught William some wrestling moves. He also sold Jacob and William a couple books, although there were several more that William would have latched on to if money wasn't so scarce. Jacob bought a copy of the The Navigator by Zadok Cramer which had just been published that year. The Navigator provided instructions and precautions for traveling west along the riverways. It really didn't come as a surprise to Sarah who had sensed that hunger in Jacob again to see more of the newer territory. Just a matter of time, she mused, before he would bring up the idea of traveling further west.

William was allowed to purchase one book and, after much deliberation, settled upon The Journal of David Brainard written by Jonathon Edwards. Uncle Zeb had shared with William the wonderful adventures as well as extraordinary trials David Brainard had experienced as a missionary to the American Indians back in the mid-1700s. The book so intrigued William that he feverishly read it and was nearly finished when Zeb stopped by for his final visit before heading back East. "I've never seen a boy as hungry as you for such things," Zeb bellowed loudly as William described to his uncle some things he had learned from Brainard's journal. "You remind me a lot of that fellow Asbury, the circuit-riding preacher."

"Who's that, Uncle Zeb?" an inquisitive William asked.

"You mean you haven't heard of Francis Asbury? I figured as religious as your folks are getting that you all would have heard of him by now," Zeb replied. "From New England to the Carolinas, and from the Atlantic to here in Kentucky, this Methodist preacher rides horseback in pursuit of souls," Zeb quoted from memory a line out of an article he had penned in an eastern publication several months back. "I was told that the man is so devoted that he talks folks into tying him to the saddle when he is too sick to ride himself. They say he's a bit frail and frequently sick but he's got some kind of drive! These circuit-riding preachers travel a route anywhere from two hundred to five hundred miles every two to six weeks preaching and starting churches. I wrote a piece or two on them last year. People sure seem to be interested in their spirit!" Zeb expounded. "I actually found that half of these circuit riders died before age thirty, and yet more keep signing up! My guess is that these revival meetings are going to produce even more of them," Zeb concluded.

William couldn't sleep that night. Something seemed to be burning inside of him and consuming his whole being. *A circuit-riding preacher,* he thought to himself. "Sharing the good news of Jesus to those spreading out across this new land," he whispered out loud. "God, please use me! I want to see people saved. Lord, help me become a circuit-riding preacher."

CHAPTER 9
GOING WEST

Logan County, KY, Spring 1806

Life for the Travers had been good on the Gaspar River, but it had become evident to all that Pa was restless. The itching to move on wasn't because Jacob was unhappy. He had a good shoe-making business, was a deacon at the Gaspar River church, had a nice cabin with forty acres of good land along the river, and most of all he had a fine family that loved and respected him. What spurred him on was a hunger to see what was over the next mountain and past the next prairie. After the United States purchased the Louisiana Territory back in '03 his spirit of adventure had hit a peak level. Pa bent the ear of anyone who would discuss Lewis and Clark's trek up the Missouri River, as well as what Zebulon Pike would find as he headed west into the great unknown.

A letter arrived for Jacob one day in early 1806 from one of the families from the Gaspar River congregation who had headed to the Upper Louisiana Territory across the Mississippi River about six months earlier. One family had settled near Sainte Genevieve and another along the Whitewater River, west of Cape Girardeau—both settlements in the new territory being called "Missouri" by some. "The soil is rich, the scenery spectacular and the opportunities are endless," wrote Mr. Sanders, who had been a dreamer just like Pa. That settled it for Pa, he had waited long enough and the unknown was calling to him. Mr. Sanders supplied Jacob with details on the area, the route he took, and the name of Barthelimi Cousin who assisted new settlers in acquiring land and permits in the Cape Girardeau area.

Because their heart beat with the same passion, William and John talked with their pa about the West more than anyone else. Although Sarah wasn't necessarily against the idea of moving again, it was clear that her men were to be held back no longer, so she put up little fight; her only reluctance was that Jacob preferred to leave now rather than waiting for summer.

Four mules purchased for the trip were hitched up to the wagon with the boys loading the last of their belongings. Sarah stood facing the cabin with tears in her eyes.

Jacob, noticing his wife's distress, walked over to her and wrapped his arm around her in consolation. "We'll build you an even bigger and better one in Missouri," Pa whispered.

"It's not the cabin so much," Sarah uttered brokenly as she wiped her eyes. "We've raised the boys here," she paused to keep her voice from cracking, "so many good memories."

William and John came up quietly and stood by Ma, also remembering the good times they had shared at the home place.

"Why don't you offer a prayer for our family, William, and for a safe journey," Jacob said softly as he laid a hand on William's shoulder. William had grown so much, both physically and spiritually, and it had become obvious to Jacob and Sarah over the last few years that William had a call on his life. His hunger for the things of God and his humble spirit had endeared him to Pastor McGready and other ministers in the area who had invested much in the young disciple. All felt that William would some day be a minister himself if the Lord willed it.

After prayer, the rocking and creaking wagon made its way down the trail and out of sight of the home they had loved.

The solemnity gave way to excitement as the wagon forded its first creek and talk of the West once again filled the morning air. However, the Travers family was under no illusions as to the challenges they would face on their journey. Their journey meant exposure to the elements, braving the storms, and possible encounters with thieves and wild animals. Traveling in the spring introduced another challenge in that spring rains can swell the waterways. Pa and Ma had discussed this at length but Pa was convinced that the trek Mr. Sanders had provided him would be passable even if the water level was higher than usual. Arriving in the Missouri Territory before summer would allow them time to set up a homestead and put in crops. At the start of each day Sarah would fry up bacon and the family would eat bacon and corn bread before heading the team back out on the trail. Jacob and Sarah rode in the wagon while William and John each rode horses. If all went well they might make fifteen miles a day. Riding up ahead as evening drew close, William would search out a campsite for the night. Each evening, John and William would gather up wood for a camp fire as Sarah made preparations for supper. The men would take turns guarding the livestock and their belongings throughout the night so as to prevent any scavengers, both the four-legged and the two-legged kind, from surprising them.

One mid-morning, a week into their journey, they rolled up to a river that was attempting to overflow its banks. The thundershower through the night had them worried for the rain poured down for a good two hours straight.

The family sat in silence as Jacob considered the situation. The river was no more than fifty yards across at the crossing but it widened and deepened not more than twenty yards downstream. To make matters worse there was already a good deal of jagged driftwood filling up on the opposite end of the crossing. If the team and wagon could not maintain it's footing and was swept downstream much at all, then the mules risked getting tangled in the driftwood and potentially spilling the wagon.

Jacob prayed quietly to himself, not only feeling the weight of responsibility for the safety and well-being of his family, but driven by that inward stubbornness to plow through regardless of the difficulty. If he had been alone he felt confident that he would have proceeded in spite of the circumstances.

Sarah interrupted his thoughts, "Jacob, are you sure we can make it across?"

"I'll take Bess and test the waters a little bit," Jacob replied seriously.

He mounted one of the horses and began wading out into the current. It was obvious why this spot had been chosen for a crossing because the ground was solid and the depth was not more than a foot to a foot-and-a-half at the center even though the water level was elevated. The swiftness of the current and the debris were still a concern but Jacob seemed to make a decision after having ridden Bess successfully over and back again.

"The ground is solid and the team is strong; I'm sure we can make it," Jacob stated assuredly. His confidence seemed to energize the boys so Sarah complied, although still visibly apprehensive and nervous. "Let's go, mules, ya, mules!" Jacob yelled as he gave the ones in the rear a crack of the whip to get them moving. The team began making its way across the muddy waterway with William riding behind the wagon on his mount with John up ahead on Bess. The team moved slowly, but steadily, along the crossing without seeming to drift. John was across now and had turned watching the progress.

Suddenly, one of the front mules got spooked from a piece of driftwood that brushed its leg and gave a kick and a jump. This startled the other mules, and the whole team shifted several feet downstream. Jacob began to yell excitably, making swift action of his whip, but the team had lost their footing and was drifting more and more towards the pile of driftwood to the left. William saw the situation deteriorating rapidly and acted quickly.

Moving his horse up alongside the front right mule, William threw a loop over its neck and tied the rope tightly around his pommel. He began to pull the mule back upstream; providing the animals precious moments needed to regain their footing. Slowly the team plodded through the remaining fifteen yards or so to the bank, trembling slightly from the intense experience.

The remainder of the trip to Cape Girardeau was relatively uneventful. Although not as dramatic as their experience the week before, William's heart beat rapidly as they crossed the Great River, the Mississippi. Mr. Sanders had described their crossing as a major affair in his letter to Pa. Their wagon had been disassembled and the wagon pieces and their belongings shipped over by pirogue little by little—taking nearly half a day. Someone had since made a scow, a large flat boat that ferried the Travers and their covered wagon across the river without a great deal of difficulty. The scow was fitted with big blocks of wood to hold the wagon securely as the men maneuvered the watercraft across the muddy river. His heart raced with excitement, for this river represented, at least in his mind, the entering of the West. What adventures awaited him and his family there?

William pulled the gift he had received from Komoka out of his pocket and began running his fingers over it. Would he ever see his Indian friend again? Komoka's father had said that they too were crossing the Great River to go into the Upper Louisiana Territory. How long ago had it been? Some eight years now, he supposed. Mostly, he wondered if the Lord would open a door for him to pursue his dream of becoming a circuit-riding preacher to the people spreading across this grand new expanse.

"I wonder," he whispered aloud, totally unaware of the wave of water splashing up on his feet, for his mind was already exploring the land on which he would soon set foot.

CHAPTER 10
CAPE GIRARDEAU

Upper Louisiana Territory, Spring 1806

"Cape Girardeau was just laid out as a town in February of this year," Barthelimi Cousin explained excitedly as he was working on paperwork for the Travers family. "I guess I should know," he chuckled to himself and then looked up smiling broadly, "because I was the one that did it!" He patted Jacob on the back and gave out a big laugh before continuing with the permit. "Louis Lorimier, he pretty much owns the whole town. He has been here since '93 and I guess you might say he is the founder," Barthelimi continued.

The Frenchman had such a jovial manner that William couldn't help but smile just listening to the man talk. William learned within the first fifteen minutes of their discussion with Monsieur Cousin that he was one of the few French settlers in Cape Girardeau. Sainte Genevieve, which was a few miles further up river, was primarily a French community but it was mostly Americans who were settling in these parts. And yes, there were several Indians around, mostly the Delaware and the Shawnee. Lorimier was very friendly with the Indians and was instrumental in bringing in many of the Delaware and Shawnee, who were not really native to this region. It seems that some years back the Spanish, who had once owned and controlled the Upper Louisiana Territory, were having some troubles with the Osage Indians. It was their hope that the Delaware and Shawnee, who were friendly with the white man, would serve as a sort of barrier between them and the ever-volatile Osage.

"There have been several Delaware Indians converted by Moravian missionaries so many folks call them the "Christian Indian" since many

43

of the other tribes have been quite resistant to the gospel message," Barthelimi had replied when William quizzed him on the faith of the Indians. William felt that familiar stir as the discussion turned to spiritual matters.

Over all, the region was raw and wild, and Sunday services were rare. There were more and more folks moving in from Kentucky, Illinois, and Tennessee who were good Christian people, but there was little organization when it came to religion this side of the Mississippi. Barthelimi explained that in Sainte Genevieve and up around Saint Louis there was more of a Catholic presence, but he was unaware of much Protestant work in the area.

"Oh Lord," William prayed quietly to himself, "open doors for us to minister here. May the gospel go forth to the white man, black man, and red man alike; use me, Lord Jesus."

The Travers family rolled out of town with the deed to forty acres of prime farm ground along the Whitewater River some fifteen miles or so west of Cape Girardeau. A great deal of joy and laughter enveloped the family as they soaked in the beauty of the rolling hills and lush countryside. Farms were scattered throughout the fifteen mile stretch to the banks of the Whitewater River but there was still plenty of wide open land.

"It is breathtaking isn't it," Ma said as the wagon topped a ridge overlooking the river valley.

Jacob pulled the team to a stop and placed his arm around Sarah, "We're home...this just feels like home."

John turned toward William with a sly grin on his face, "Bet I can beat ya to the river!" he exclaimed as he gave Bess a kick.

William's grin widened as he kicked his horse and took off after him. The two were neck and neck as they approached the banks of the river. A brief glance over at William made it clear to John that his brother did not mean to give up. The two boys continued kicking their horses and yelling until at last they both jumped their horses right off of the bank into the rippling flow of water. Flying over their horse's heads, both boys landed head first into the water. They came up laughing and slapping each other, while all along failing to notice the young boy sitting along the water's edge with a fishing pole in his hand. William spotted him first.

"Oh, hey there…we didn't know anyone was here."

The boy was taken aback by the abrupt arrival of these two young men, and somewhat shocked by the dramatic end to their race. It wasn't until the brothers had made their way over to the boy that he finally found his voice.

"I'm Billy, Billy Randol. I live a couple ridges over that way," he stammered as he pointed back towards the northeast.

Billy's eyes were still wide with surprise and it struck John so funny that he let out a burst of laughter. "I guess we did look pretty funny," William said as he began laughing loudly himself.

Finally Billy got over his shock and began to giggle along with them.

Jacob and Sarah made their way to the river bank in the wagon, and Sarah, being all worked up, was ready to scold the boys until she caught sight of Billy.

Whatever words she had begun to speak were choked back and what came forth instead was, "Well hello young man; what might your name be?"

It took Billy a moment to regain composure, but he finally managed to repeat his name and, once again, pointed out the direction of his home.

"Looks like we are to be neighbors then Mr. Billy Randol," Jacob said. "We'll be looking forward to meeting your folks."

It wasn't long before Billy brought his parents, John and Mary, back to meet the Travers. It was almost immediately apparant that the Randol family was a gift from heaven. Mary brought some fresh baked bread and John was carrying a couple chickens as a welcome gift. A couple days later, John Randol arrived with some other men from the area and together with Jacob, William, and John they began building a log home. The many experienced hands sped the job along, and before long two square pens were completed. Between them was an open space about as large as one of the pens. A single roof spanned the length of the two pens and extended far enough in the front and rear to form porches. The cracks between the logs forming the house were filled with mud and each pen had two doors.

"The space between the two rooms is left open for the circulation of light and air," Mr. Randol explained when William questioned him about it.

William took to Mr. Randol right away and sensed a deep love in the man. The man's knowledge and easy manner impressed William as well. After the other men had left, they talked for a good hour, and it came as no surprise to William that Mr. Randol brought up spiritual matters in the discussion.

"I was sure you were a Christian!" William exclaimed as he began to relate his experiences back at the Gaspar River church. William was thrilled to learn that the Randol family was a part of a group of Methodists who had just recently organized a church a few miles east of their home.

That evening, after everyone had returned to their own homes, the Travers family had a time of prayer and thanksgiving for the Lord leading them to this particular place and providing them such good and godly neighbors.

"God's mercies are new every morning," Jacob exclaimed as he closed the prayer time.

CHAPTER 11
FRUIT OF BITTERNESS

Castor River, Upper Louisiana Territory, Spring 1806

For the two and half years since the loss of their son by Indian attack, Harrison had grown even more bitter towards the red man and looked for any and all opportunities to rid the territory of their existence. What tribe they were from or what allowances were given them by the government made no difference to him. For Vera and Laura, life had lost its luster. Although they also felt the deep loss of a beloved son and brother, it was their state of existence at home with Harrison that drained the life right out of them. His hatred and bitterness had not only driven him to drink, but had vented itself in emotional abuse to those whom he loved most.

Harrison, like several of the locals who worked in the mines, would take some time off during the spring to focus on farming. The community of St. Michael, which was about seven miles southwest of their home on Castor River and five miles south of the mines at La Motte where Harrison worked, was beginning to grow and a local merchant had set up shop to sell seed, flour, sugar, some linen, and other basic commodities.[3] Besides farming and mining, trading and transportation were becoming the more predominant industries in the Upper Louisiana Territory. A couple merchants sent a team and wagon from the new territory all the way to Baltimore; a trip taking about three months. Others made use of the Great River by shipping goods to New Orleans. A trip from Sainte Genevieve to New Orleans would take from twenty five to thirty days, whereas the

---

3 Historical note: St. Michael was renamed Fredericktown in 1819 and relocated a short distance north of the original site.

return trip upstream could take up to four months. Nonetheless, all was endeavored for the sake of progress.

Vera and Laura, always eager to visit with other women folk, persuaded Harrison to take them along on his trip to St. Michael to buy seed and some other staples. They were also excited to visit the merchant, Mr. Stan Bernbaum, of which they had only heard about from Harrison as he made a trip to St. Michael every couple months or so.

They arrived in the young community an hour after sunrise and were warmly greeted by the heavyset merchant behind the counter. "Welcome Mr. Smith, good to see you! So I finally get to meet your lovely wife and charming daughter," he bellowed, a wide grin across his face.

Laura noticed two things right off about this jovial fellow in front of her; first, his smile was contagious and she couldn't help but to return the gesture of kindness. She was sure that she couldn't have kept her face from smiling even if she had a mind to. This man just had a demeanor about him that tickled her heart. The second thing she noticed was the man's hands—they were enormous! He had extended his hand to shake hers and the moment that Laura took his hand it was as if her hand had been completed swallowed by his.

"What can I get for you folks this fine morning? Oh, just so you know, the wife has some fresh preserves here…made them not more than a day ago," the merchant said as he pointed to several jars on the counter.

When was the last time I tasted preserves on a fresh piece of bread, Laura thought to herself, staring at the jar. She saw right off that her ma was thinking the same thing as she picked up a jar, raised it to her nose and took a long, satisfying smell.

"We won't be needing any of that," Harrison stated sharply as he gave a hard look to Vera.

Vera quickly replaced the jar of preserves to its proper place, lowering her head.

Without delay Harrison began sharing his list with the merchant while Laura and her ma made their way around the small store quietly admiring the marvelous treasures—at least to them. Calico was priced at a dollar a yard, linen for seventy-five cents a yard, pins were thirty-one and a fourth cents a paper, note paper was fifty cents a quire and even some silk bonnets.

"Books, Ma" Laura whispered to her ma as she found a handful of books and magazines in a box. Delighted, she started fingering through the titles. Ever since her ma had read her that first bedtime story, she had been fascinated by the written page. After learning to read, she savored every occasion she had to lose herself in some romantic adventure. In part, she simply loved to read, and she treasured these escapes as a way to retreat from her personal misery at home. It was not that she hated her father, she mostly pitied him. Not only was he miserable, but he made everyone around him miserable as well. Hate was destroying him—and his family.

Laura was deeply engrossed in a novel about a prince in a foreign land when a man in buckskin with a pile of furs over his shoulder made his way to the counter.

"Ah Jim, I see you've been doing some trading with your Indian friends again," Mr. Bernbaum said as he began picking through the pile of furs.

Harrison's reaction was immediate and forceful, causing the merchant to take a step back, "Indians! You get these furs from Indians?"

"I do a bit of trappin' myself," Jim stated flatly with a hard gaze at Harrison, "but I've found it a bit more profitable to do some tradin' with the injuns, seeing as they can get a lot more of them in a shorter amount of time. For some trinkets and little bit of whiskey I can get all this," he finished while patting the pile of furs.

Laura moved over next to her ma who placed her arm around Laura. They both braced themselves for the storm that was about to hit.

"I can't abide those filthy Indians and neither can I abide any man who would do business with them," Harrison snarled as he turned to face this new focus of his hatred.

Obviously no stranger to such situations, the man was more than ready to respond accordingly to this obvious challenge. Without a word, Jim brought his right hand up from his side with such swiftness that Harrison was taken totally off guard. The fist connected with his jaw, turning him around and knocking him up against some barrels. Harrison himself was not unaccustomed to an occasional brawl—especially in the last couple of years as his quick temper and sharp tongue initiated more than a few such interactions. However, this was the first time that Vera and Laura had the misfortune to witness it firsthand.

"Harrison!" Vera screamed as Laura began running to her dad.

Harrison was still game and, pushing Laura back, started in with raised fists. Frantically moving delicate items out of the way, the merchant yelled at the men to take it outside.

Jim smiled as Harrison moved in, for this was old hat to him. Harrison swung a wide right at Jim's head but Jim dodged it and countered with his left. The punch caught Harrison on the ear but he was moving in like a bull and seemed unhurt by the blow.

Harrison wrapped his arms around his opponent and began to squeeze with all his might. The man pushed off of the counter, causing Harrison to lose his footing and loosen his hold for an instant.

Making the most of the opportunity, Jim shoved his elbow hard into Harrison's mid-section, knocking the wind out of him. Then turning swiftly, he landed another right on Harrison's jaw, knocking him to the floor.

Harrison struggled to get up, slightly disoriented. Vera ran over to her husband and helped him to his feet.

"I'm truly sorry ma'am but I've never been one to cotton to such foolish talk," Jim said sheepishly. "I sure regret this whole affair. Maybe some day I'll learn to just walk away," the man said softly, then turned and walked out the door.

Later that evening, with the family back at their cabin on the Castor River, Laura sat alone under an oak tree with the family Bible lying open in her lap. As much as she loved to read, she had avoided reading the Scriptures the last couple of years for she felt that God had abandoned their family. The loss of her brother and the situation with her dad had fostered anger in her that she did not know how to deal with. The most logical person to blame, in her opinion, had been God. Why had he allowed Jed to be killed by Indians? Why did her dad take out his pain and anger on her and her mom? Would she ever be free from these fears and uncertainties? Would she ever find love—would she be able to love?

"God, please help me. I can't handle this on my own anymore," she prayed as a tear rolled down her cheek onto the Bible.

Her eyes drifted to the wet spot on the page. *"Why art thou cast down, O my soul? And why art thou disquieted in me? Hope thou in God: for I shall yet praise him for the help of his countenance."*[4]

---

4 Psalm 42:5.

CHAPTER 12
PREACHER ON TRIAL

Cape Girardeau District 1810

The last four years had flown by for the Travers family as they assimilated quickly into their new life on the sunset side of the Mississippi. They had begun attending the Methodist church with the Randol family and had made several new friends among the faithful there.

William, now twenty-two years old, had only recently applied for the opportunity to become a preacher on trial with the Methodist movement. Jesse Walker, the Methodist circuit-riding preacher, was appointed to the Cape Girardeau circuit in 1809 after having served on another Missouri circuit back in 1807 (a circuit that embraced all of the settlements north of the Meramec River and along the Missouri River). Jesse had become quite fond of William and the two spent as much time together as Jesse could manage with his busy schedule. Moreover, he shared with William how the Upper Louisiana Territory had only officially opened up to the Methodist church in 1806 when John Travis was appointed to Missouri. His instructions were "to find people, organize classes, locate and arrange for regular preaching places, and to be the gatherer of a widely scattered flock."

William McKendree, presiding elder of the Cumberland District, which included Missouri, made a tour of the Upper Louisiana Territory in the summer of 1807. Geographically, the district was enormous and the settlements were, for the most part, widely scattered making the new territory an awesome challenge. McKendree had a vision for the vast region and his tireless travels greatly encouraged the people and inspired the preachers to yet greater action. The Cape Girardeau circuit was the fourth circuit launched in Upper Louisiana, but Jesse Walker was not the only servant of the Lord sowing seed in the Cape Girardeau area. Elder Samuel Parker came to Cape Girardeau in 1809 and began the organization of a church in the small river town. Along with a third Methodist preacher, Thomas Wright, plans were now underway for the first camp meeting in the Cape Girardeau area.

William's heart was pounding and his palms were sweaty as he finished buttoning his vest and combed his hair. This day had been a long time in coming, but he was finally taking the first big step toward realizing his dream. How old had he been when he first felt the Holy Spirit tugging at his heart to become a minister of the gospel? He was twelve years old the night of the Red River communion service when he had seen an image of himself among many saints of God spreading the gospel across the western territory. And it was Uncle Zeb, of all people, that God had used to plant that seed in his heart about the circuit-riding preacher. The feeling he had on that first night as he prayed was just as real today, if not burning even brighter.

"Today's the day," Sarah said, surprising William and causing him to jump.

"Oh, you startled me...I was just thinking," William said with a nervous smile.

"You were a million miles away," Sarah breathed as she began straightening William's string bowtie.

"Yeah, it's hard to believe that it's really happening. I've been dreaming about it for so long and I...I don't want to mess anything up today," William sighed as he nervously fiddled with his vest again.

Sarah lifted William's chin so that their eyes met. "You listen to me William Travers, it is God who put this desire in your heart to be a preacher and nothing of yourself or anyone else," she stated strongly but lovingly. "Since it was God who called you, He will be with you and His will is going to win the day," she continued as she smoothed a stray hair on his forehead. "Now you know Jesse Walker and Elder Parker are very fond of you. These men love God just as you do and they are going to be sensitive to His voice. You just go into that meeting with your head high and share from your heart," she finished with a smile and a pat on his chest.

"Yes ma'am," William replied, hugging his ma.

Elder Samuel Parker as well as his friend Jesse Walker were both present to conduct the interview when William entered the room. His application to become a "preacher on trial" with the Methodist church had been received and reviewed; all that remained was today's interview.

Jesse smiled and rose from his seat when William entered the room. "Well I see you made it…I thought maybe you'd changed your mind," Jesse grinned from ear to ear as he took William's hand. William couldn't help but laugh, which helped to drain a good bit of the tenseness right out of him.

Elder Parker smiled as well, rising from his chair and extending his hand to William. "Relax son, this isn't going to hurt…too badly," he said as his smile widened, wrinkling his eyes.

The three men seated themselves and Elder Parker opened their meeting with a word of prayer.

"William we have watched you closely over the last year and were not at all surprised to receive your application to join our ranks," Elder Parker began. "It has been quite obvious to Brother Walker and me that the Lord has His hand on you, and furthermore, you have consistently exemplified the characteristics of Christ and the qualities we are looking for in our circuit-riding preachers," he continued. "We have read your testimony of the Lord's dealing with you and this is of utmost importance since it's ultimately the call of God that is key. We have learned over the course of our ministry that it's not always those that seem most equipped that are effective in service. Rather, God seems to delight in equipping those whom He has called. We have the distinct advantage here today of having interacted with you in many different situations and settings, and thus have seen the evidence of your call. Nevertheless, for the sake of protocol and for the satisfaction of our superiors we would like to go over the four questions that are required for each candidate offering himself for the circuit riding ministry."

"Number one," Elder Parker continued, "is this man truly converted?"

"Here, here," Jesse piped in, again smiling broadly.

"Yes," Elder Parker agreed, "William has accepted Jesus Christ as his Lord and Savior which is evidenced by his life. Number two, does he know and keep our rules? I understand from Brother Walker that he has given you a copy of the *Methodist Book of Discipline* and has assured me that you have become quite familiar with it," Elder Parker stated.

"Yes, Elder Parker," William replied, "I have many of them committed to memory and have been making a very conscious effort to keep them all."

"Number three," Elder Parker continued, "can he preach acceptably?"

Jesse Walker crossed his legs and cleared his throat, "The boy will do. I have heard him preach on at least three occasions and he brings it down where the people are. He uses good examples of everyday life to illustrate his points and most of all the boy is anointed when he is behind the pulpit. It is obvious to me that he takes it very seriously and prepares well both in his study and in prayer," Jesse concluded.

"Does he appear to be swatting bees as he is preaching like another minister I know?" asked Elder Parker, lowering his glasses on his nose as he glanced over at Jesse with a twinkle in his eye. Jesse just rolled his eyes as William grinned.

"Finally, number four," Elder Parker said, "has he a horse?"

"Yes sir, Pa has agreed to let me have Ol' Bess since she is steady as the sun and strong as an ox…that's quoting my pa of course," William said.

"Son, your horse is your biggest asset outside of your Bible and the Holy Spirit," Elder Parker said passionately. "Take good care of your horse. Ride moderately and see to it yourself that your horse is rubbed down and fed."

Elder Parker concluded, "As presiding elder in this district I am accepting your application to become a circuit-riding preacher on trial with the Methodist church and hereby confer upon you the title of Reverend William Travers. By the way, you will be expected to participate in the preaching for the upcoming camp meeting to be held on William

Williams' land.[5] This meeting is adjourned. Jesse, why don't you close us in a word of prayer."

Elder Parker and Jesse Walker both laid their hands on William as Jesse prayed aloud asking God's richest anointing on William and for him to be mightily used of God in bringing many lost souls into the kingdom.

After the prayer, William stood to his feet, thanked the men of God and headed for the door. As he walked outside a wave of relief washed over him and he let out an audible sigh as he bowed his head in thanksgiving, "Thank you, Lord, for your goodness to me. Please help me be the best circuit-riding preacher I can be."

Men had worked for about three days preparing the site for the upcoming camp meeting. Excitement was high seeing how several of the families had experienced at least one camp meeting on the east side of the Great River before coming West. William and his family reminisced about the meetings at the Red River church and how the Lord had moved mightily that last day. Sarah recalled with enthusiasm the unity displayed by the different denominations while Jacob reminded them of that heavy set lady that squealed like a pig when she sang. As before, Jacob received a swift and sound slapping from his wife for his impertinence. John recalled the wonderful music which he had so enjoyed. In fact, he had learned to play some fiddle himself since their move to Missouri and had grown accustomed to playing every time they gathered for worship. With earnest prayer William sought the Lord's direction for the message God would have him share and for His anointing on the services.

Finally, the day arrived and the Travers family took their place on the plank seats that had been made specifically for the occasion. Elder Parker opened the meeting with prayer and Brother Randol led the people in a couple of songs.

---

5 Historical Note: William Williams moved to Missouri from Kentucky in 1801. A devout Methodist, he set aside two acres of his farm for use as a camp meeting around the date proposed in this book. Several years later a church was built on this spot (1819) and was fully restored in the early 1920s, making it one of the oldest Protestant houses of worship still standing west of the Mississippi. This Heritage Landmark of the United Methodist Church, Old McKendree Chapel, is located near Jackson, MO.

A feeling of disappointment crept over William as he looked around. He had hoped for a great turnout since they had publicized the event all around the Cape Girardeau district. However, not more than a few dozen folks were there and very few making their way in. Nevertheless, Jesse Walker, when he took the pulpit to bring the first message of the camp meeting, preached as if there were five hundred present—swatting bees the whole time. Preaching truly energized Jesse and he was notorious for swinging his arms, running, and spitting. Even so, the people loved it and got caught up in the fervor of his message. William was not near as animated in his preaching but, young though he was, he connected with the common man.

William was given the second preaching slot during the meeting and had prepared to preach about Samson from the book of Judges. For his introduction he shared an analogy. "Let me introduce you to my horse, Ol' Bess," William began as he pointed to an imaginary horse next to him. "I feed my horse oats regularly so that she will be healthy and strong. However, times are changing and oats are more expensive than they used to be," William said. "I'm finding it more difficult to buy the oats so I've come up with an idea. I'm going to mix in a little bit of sawdust along with the oats," William said as he mimicked feeding the horse. "Well, it looks like the little bit of sawdust didn't hurt my horse none so I'm gonna add a little more sawdust and a little less oats," William continued while once again pretending to feed the horse.

The scene continued as William explained that he added more and more sawdust while removing more and more of the oats. Finally, he explained that since he has seen no negative repercussions from swapping out oats with sawdust he would simply feed his horse straight sawdust. Then William conjured up a shocked and sorrowful expression and explained that Ol' Bess just collapsed and died. "Folks, this is what happens when we get comfortable with sin. Little by little we compromise our stance against sin and give in to temptation. Sin destroys and eventually we are the loser."

"Samson now," William continued, "had great potential. A man mightily used of God, but lacking discipline and true dedication. Lust and selfishness began replacing godly characteristics to the point that the Spirit left him and *"he wist not that the Lord was departed from him."* Retelling the story of Samson, he highlighted the dangers of playing with sin.

Although nervous when he had taken the pulpit, the anointing of the Holy Spirit and the affirmation from his friends and family in the crowd during the message settled him right down so that he felt at ease during the message.

Jesse smiled to himself as William gave an appeal at the end of his message. The boy had a unique style about him. He couldn't help but think of how Jesus used parables to relate to the common people. Similarly, William was able to convey the message in ways the people could understand.

"That'll do son," he commended William, patting him on the back as he joined him to pray for those who had come forward.

CHAPTER 13
LEARNING THE ROPES

Cape Girardeau Circuit, Summer 1810

Being a "preacher on trial" gave William the opportunity to travel with Jesse Walker on his regular circuit. Their normal day consisted of 4:00 a.m. prayer time and Bible reading, followed by a quick breakfast of corn dodgers and a cup of coffee before hitting the saddle. In this new territory all of the circuits were rural with the average circumference being from two hundred to five hundred miles, taking anywhere from two to six weeks to complete. The Cape Girardeau circuit took about four weeks and consisted of preaching appointments nearly every day. Meetings took place in homes, barns, open air, schoolhouses, and occasionally in the meeting house of another denomination.

"Never despise small beginnings," Jesse had said when they pulled reign at their first stop on the circuit.

An elderly man in homespun britches and no shoes or shirt stepped out from his one room shack and greeted them warmly. Although the man was obviously very poor he was eager to offer his guests some corn bread and sassafras tea. William started to refuse but Jesse touched his arm and made it clear from his facial expression that it was important to accept his kind gesture.

After sharing in a time of small talk and sipping tea, the older man rose from the table and pulled out his worn Bible from off of a shelf. A warmth filled William's heart as he watched the frail man follow along in his Bible while Jesse shared from the Scriptures. Following a time of prayer, the gentleman sincerely thanked them and stood waving for several minutes until they rode out of sight.

Most of their many stops were such as this where perhaps one to twelve of God's precious flock would be assembled to open the Scripture together. A couple of stops were in small communities where a weekly class convened. Oftentimes, they were led by a layman who could barely read but had been under the teaching of a minister for a season sometime in his lifetime. It was always a joy for them to receive the circuit-riding preacher who administered Communion to them and spent some time with them in the Scriptures. As their thirst for the Word was not quickly quenched, it was not uncommon to spend three to four hours with these folks.

Of course William soon learned that the circuit-rider's life was not all peaches and cream. Although he had heard the stories of sleeping on the hard, cold ground, wild animal encounters, interactions with the rougher element, and those who were down right cruel, it never really rings true until one lives it. It was not that William hadn't prepared himself for it as much as a person could, but reality has a way of knocking the wind right out of a person.

About the time they were into the third week of their circuit, the jerked beef was losing its appeal for William. Occasionally, there was a meal with a family along the circuit, but he couldn't help but miss his ma's good home cookin' and the comfort of having three square meals a day. The first week had also held his awe with sleeping under the stars but then the reality of the hard ground and slithering creatures began to take their toll on his back and attitude. One morning he had awakened to find a rather large snake laying at his feet—at least it seemed large to him at the time. Jesse got a big kick out of his high-pitched scream and quick retreat.

But the thing that troubled William the most was their encounter with Mr. Bart Starlin. That was a name he was quite sure he would never forget—nor would he forget those eyes. Jesse explained how he often tried to stake out potential additions to his route by either asking his regulars of any new families that had moved in or by simply varying his route slightly to explore new areas. It was the latter that had taken them to a little cabin several miles from any community, or other cabin for that matter. They had seen the smoke from a few miles away and decided to make a visit. At the edge of the homestead they stopped and yelled out a greeting so as not to come up on someone suddenly and thereby risk getting shot. A bear of a man with a large black beard stepped out from the cabin with rifle in hand. "What in the sam hill do you want…what are you doing on my property?" he bellowed, walking briskly towards them while raising his rifle. His boorish demeanor along with his harsh response alarmed William causing him to feel a sudden urge to turn his horse and run.

Jesse raised his hands and spoke quickly but calmly to the big, burly man. "We mean you no harm mister. We are Methodist clergy making a circuit through these parts and saw your smoke a few miles east of here. We were in hopes we could interest you in some good Christian fellowship," Jesse shared sincerely.

"I got no interest in your Christian talk or your crazy beliefs," the man screamed holding his rifle on Jesse. "Bart Starlin ain't no fool and I won't be bewitched by that fool book of yours either. You just get before I bury you where you stand."

William was hypnotized by the man's eyes. When he had come as close as ten feet from them, William could see that his face was almost entirely covered with hair and those eyes appeared to reach out and grab him. They were crazy eyes, like those of a lobo wolf.

Jesse did not hesitate but stated quickly, "We meant no harm sir and we'll leave right away."

Jesse motioned for William to follow as he turned his mount and walked slowly back the way they had come, not daring to look back. William could almost feel the icy stare of the giant man on his back as they walked their horses over the ridge and out of sight.

"I hope that doesn't happen very often," William said when they had ridden a good mile or so. His stomach still felt a queer burning sensation and he couldn't seem to get that image of the man's eyes out of his head.

"Unfortunately William, there are some ornery folks out there but for the most part people will show respect to a preacher," Jesse replied. "This is a rough land and it can breed some rough characters. I remember one time over in Illinois when I was preaching in a schoolhouse. A couple of children were sitting in the gathering who I had assumed belonged to a young mother that was present. We weren't fifteen minutes into the meeting when a tall, barrel-chested man stormed into the schoolhouse and grabbed up the two children and turned to face me. With his finger in my face the man yelled, 'I'll have no worthless Bible-thumper brain-washing my kids. The next time I see you spouting your poison around my children I'm gonna close that mouth of yours for good,' he threatened then ushered his children out the door. That's rare, although it is not uncommon to have drunks interrupt meetings or some ruffians pull out their guns and fire a couple shots then ride off," Jesse continued.

"Most folks are respectful even if they don't share our beliefs. I've found that most of the homesteaders in these parts are so hungry for company and news from back East that they will feed you and hear you out just to fill that void they have," Jesse said. "It's an adventure son," Jesse concluded as he reached over and slapped William on the back.

CHAPTER 14
IN SEARCH OF A NEW CIRCUIT

New Madrid District, Early Fall 1810

The air was beginning to have a hint of crispness as it blew through the willows. Three men sat around a campfire in a willow grove sharing yarns and drinking coffee. John Scripps, an energetic young man from the Cape Girardeau church, stared up at the stars between sips of his coffee.

"Isn't it a clear and peaceful night?" he asked.

John was about the same age as William and had been showing interest in the ministry as well; being somewhat familiar with the area, he was eager to offer his assistance on the trip.

William and Jesse leaned back and gazed up at the heavens as well.

"To think, the One who placed all of the stars in place now lives in our heart," Jesse marveled.

The three men were not simply enjoying an evening out under the stars, but were on a mission. Elder Parker had passed on the news that another circuit was to be explored down toward the expanding settlement of New Madrid. The route they were taking was called "*El Camino Real*" by the Spanish who had opened it up in 1789. In English it means "The King's Highway." Of course the Spanish were actually not the first ones to travel this route from the Big Swamp south of Cape Girardeau to New Madrid. In fact, it was the Indians who first walked the great sandy ridge that parallels the Mississippi River. Furthermore, the Spanish also opened the road north of Cape Girardeau all the way to Saint Louis which, when you consider the entire route from Saint Louis to New Madrid, was a distance of about 180 miles.

The three were thoroughly enjoying each other's company around the campfire and the young men especially appreciated Jesse's stories. Jesse, being in a talkative mood, had been sharing story after story with them around the campfire. He had, of course, recounted several stories about his personal experiences but he also began sharing some from other circuit-riding preachers he had encountered at the annual conferences. One particular minister especially interested William, an eccentric fellow by the name of Lorenzo Dow.

"The story goes," Jesse began "that Lorenzo was staying at an inn when another guest there reported that his purse had been stolen from his room while he had been eating dinner. Since no new guests had arrived and no one had left it seemed evident to everyone that the thief was right there among them. Lorenzo, while talking with the innkeeper about the situation, stated that he could easily identify the thief. The innkeeper and especially the victim welcomed his intervention so Dow brought in a rooster and placed it in the center of the main room and proceeded to cover it with a huge kettle that had been hanging on the hearth," Jesse continued.

William and John were captivated by the story and with Jesse's animated way of telling it. *He tells stories about like he preaches*, William thought to himself.

"Dow then addressed the whole group and explained that he was going to shut out all of the light from the room," Jesse continued. "In the darkness each person present was to step forward and rub his hand on the bottom of the kettle. Dow explained that when the thief touches the kettle that the rooster will crow and the thief will be discovered! The lights were doused and each person filed forward to touch the kettle in the darkness but the rooster never crowed. Dow then calls for the lanterns to be lit and proceeds to inspect each person's hand. All but one person had a black smudge on their hand from the bottom of the kettle which was naturally covered with soot. The one with the guilty conscience had not touched the kettle for fear that the rooster would crow. Dow looked triumphantly at the innkeeper and proclaimed, 'there is your thief.'"

Well into the night the three talked, laughed, and sipped their coffee. It was a night that William would long remember.

After spending four weeks with Jesse on the Cape Girardeau circuit and now a couple of weeks into the exploration of a potential new one, William felt like he was beginning to get a feel for things. He was under no illusions, fully aware of the challenges that lay ahead. The initial shock had worn off and he was once again invigorated with the call. He realized that once the three men had successfully mapped this new circuit that he could potentially be given the route to maneuver on his own. A hint of fear touched him for there were so many things that could happen to a man alone in the wilderness. How many men had simply never returned from a trip without an explanation of their disappearance ever determined? Indian attacks were still a very real and ever-looming possibility. Sure, several tribes were friendly with the white man but there were still those who resented the white man's presence and would not think twice about counting coup if given an opportunity. There were also bandits and thieves who preferred making their living by taking it from honest, hard-working men and women rather than earning it by the sweat of their brow. Stories were rampant of river bandits who were making life miserable for the merchants and for the river men who were shipping merchandise up and down the Mississippi.

The land held no shortage of the bad element either. He had heard of more than one account of circuit riders being robbed while out on the trail. One circuit rider complained that when the thieves saw he had nothing but Bibles, they simply stole his shoes and horse and left him to walk barefoot to the next farmhouse. Then there were the simple accidents out in the wild whether by riding accidents or those caused by the elements. Being caught out in a severe winter storm had caused some to become disoriented and lose their way; the lucky ones were able to find shelter but there were those who were later found having frozen to death in the bitter cold. He knew his ma worried about him and yet there was still that peace in knowing that one is always the safest in the center of the Lord's will. There was also a peace in knowing that His heavenly Father was always looking out for him.

"If he can take care of the lilies and the sparrows then surely he will be mindful of me," he whispered to himself.

The traveling was slow since they were attempting to stop at as many homes and settlements as possible. The approximate boundary line between the Cape Girardeau district and the New Madrid district was understood to be Tywappity Bottoms. There were a handful of settlements along the King's Highway from Tywappity Bottoms to New Madrid such as Big Prairie.[6] Here they met Joseph Hunter and his family and enjoyed a brief, but friendly, visit. Mr. Hunter was a member of the territorial council after the transfer of the Louisiana Territory to the United States and he and his family held a prominent position in the district.

After several days of visiting settlements and homes along the way, the three riders finally made it to New Madrid. Like many of the early settlements west of the Mississippi, New Madrid was originally a trading post where white men traded with the Indians. In 1783 two French Canadian trappers and traders by the name of Francois and Joseph LeSieur founded the settlement. An interesting piece of history of this settlement concerns an American by the name of Colonel George Mason who had a vision of making New Madrid into a great city. His negotiations with the Spanish in the late 1700s are believed to be the source of the naming of the settlement New Madrid.[7] Although many of Colonel Mason's dreams were never realized, New Madrid had nonetheless become a flourishing settlement. There were about a hundred houses scattered on a fine plain two miles square; the inhabitants consisting of French Creoles, Americans, and Germans. Plenty of cattle roamed the area and cotton patches were scattered throughout the region.

The circuit-riding preachers learned much from the locals during their visit but they were somewhat disappointed as to the limited response to their requests to establish preaching points. The three continued south and visited the settlement of Little Prairie which, much to William's delight, reported a village of Delaware Indians only about

6 Historical Note: Big Prairie was near present day Sikeston.

7 Historical Note: France ceded Louisiana Territory to Spain through the Treaty of Fontainebleau in 1762 in return for Spain's assistance in the Seven Years War against England. Although French explorers and settlers continued coming into the Louisiana Territory the Spanish controlled it until 1800 when Spain agreed to transfer Louisiana to France as war indemnity. Napoleon Bonaparte agreed to sell the Louisiana Territory to the United States in 1803—$13,000,000 for 883,072 square miles.

a mile south of their settlement.[8] Although his companions were not keen on the idea of visiting the village, William determined in his heart to make a visit there if and when he was given the New Madrid circuit. The thought of seeing Komoka again was never far from his mind. All in all, their exploratory trip had been profitable in that thirty people had agreed to receive a circuit rider once one had been chosen. They all agreed, however, that there was still a great deal of work to be done to build God's kingdom in this region.

---

8 Historical Note: Little Prairie was near present day Caruthersville.

CHAPTER 15
THE WARNING

New Madrid Circuit, Late 1811

William fastened the top button on his coat and pulled his hat further down on his head. The wind had picked up and it was down right cold. Ol' Bess had grown accustomed to the New Madrid circuit route and plodded on to the next stop without any prodding. The Lord had been good and the circuit had grown, as had William. A couple of times he had stopped by the Delaware village south of Little Prairie in search of Komoka but he had yet to catch up with his old friend. He was near Little Prairie now but decided to make camp for the night.

Both by trial and error, as well as receiving good advice from others, William had also grown in regards to frontier knowledge. There was a day, not so long ago, when he would have suffered through the night with the cold and wind. Yet he had learned how to seek out the right camping site. If possible he would camp in a hollow or ravine behind some old forest tree which some storm of winter had prostrated. With his tinder-box, flint, and steel he would start a fire far enough away from the tree that his feet would be near the fire with his head and shoulders near the downed tree. He found that the heated air would curl up around the log helping to keep him warm from head to toe. He would then gather a quantity of grass, leaves, and small brush and make a soft bed for himself next to the fire. His saddle was often his pillow and with his warm blanket he rested well. A piece of jerked venison and a bit of pone with a cup of water satisfied him before curling up in his blanket.

Early the next morning, he rekindled the fire and put some coffee on before pulling out his Bible from its protective leather pouch. The Bible he had received from his Uncle Zeb several years back now was getting worn, but it held a special place in his heart so he was reluctant to replace it. He began his daily devotions and afterward sipped his coffee while enjoying the glorious sunrise. He quietly prayed to himself as he enjoyed the warm touch of the sun on his face.

Slowly but steadily, an uneasiness began to well up within him. Sitting up, he looked over one shoulder, then the other. Was it the Holy Spirit nudging him about something—a warning of some kind? William poured out the little bit of coffee that remained in his cup and set it aside. He kneeled down next to the fallen tree and began to call upon the Lord. It must have been close to an hour later that he finally felt some release but he had a strong feeling within him that the Lord was trying to prepare him for something. He rolled his bedding and made sure his fire was out then mounted up and started Ol' Bess toward Little Prairie.

William found that the ride between stops along the circuit were ideal times to read and prepare sermons so he pulled out his Bible and began reading in the Psalms.

If it hadn't been for Ol' Bess, William was sure that he would have ridden right past the Indian, even though he was standing in plain sight. William was focused on his study when he sensed a change in the horse's movement. Their long hours together on the trail had enabled both horse and rider to learn each other well. William looked up to see an Indian about forty yards away. Although he did not recognize the man, he was sure he was a Delaware and it seemed by his stare and demeanor that he was waiting for him. Even among the Delaware there are those who are dangerous so William was wary. He stopped his horse and stared back at the man, waiting to see what the Indian intended to do. William scanned the general area with his peripheral vision for other Indians while being careful not take his focus off of this man.

To his amazement the Indian slowly pulled out a sling!

Could it be? William thought to himself. "Komoka?" William ventured quizzically.

Suddenly a broad smile appeared on the chiseled face and the Indian began walking toward William. William dismounted and the two embraced.

"How my old friend?" Komoka asked.

"Very well my friend. It's so good to see you! I've been hoping to run into you...where have you been?" William asked.

"My village is good distance west but I wander much," Komoka answered. "I have been across Great River and just come from village that you visit," he continued. "They tell me you come often to Little Prairie and I ask white man at Little Prairie when you return. I am happy to find my white brother, but before we talk of family, I have important message I must speak," Komoka said solemnly as he placed a hand on William's shoulder.

"During trip on other side of Great River I make contact with Creek Indian who tell me of war party that prepare capture of Little Prairie. There is chief among Creeks who call himself Captain George and he has great hatred for white man. He has stirred up warriors to show great fight to all white men here. My brothers at village believe you can speak to someone who will listen so that good fight is made," Komoka concluded.

After a quick good-bye to his long-lost Indian friend, William wasted no time in mounting and riding to see Francois LeSieur and Captain Ruddell, who both commanded companies of militia in the area. William relayed what Komoka had told him and orders were given and preparations made to repel the attack of Indians. Scouts were sent out immediately and it didn't take them long in returning with the news that a band of Creeks had already crossed the Mississippi and were only a few miles south of Little Prairie.

The sun was beginning to disappear over the horizon when the militia began filtering along the south side of Little Prairie forming a barrier between the frightened settlers and the imminent threat. Right at sundown the scouts reported that the war party was making camp for the night. Captain Ruddell instructed the men to prepare their tents and proceeded to delegate guards for the different watches throughout the night.

Komoka slipped in next to William while he was listening to the Captain's instructions. "There will be no attack tonight," Komoka shared quietly. "They are aware of the militia's presence but they do not hesitate because of fear," he continued. "There are those who believe to be killed in the dark is to have one's soul wander forever in search of peace. I know this Indian warrior to be very clever and he will make good fight tomorrow…even now he plans," Komoka concluded. With that, Komoka turned and disappeared as quickly as he had appeared just moments before.

William prayed quietly to himself. Was this the reason for the strange feeling he had this morning? Would the battle tomorrow and the aftermath test his resolve? "Oh Lord, put a hedge of protection around us and frustrate the plans of those who would do us harm," William whispered aloud.

CHAPTER 16
EARTHQUAKE

New Madrid District, December 16, 1811

William woke suddenly to an awful noise resembling loud but distant thunder. At the same instant, the ground began to shake violently with such force that he was unable to stand. He could hear screams from the terrified inhabitants of Little Prairie among whom he had decided to pass the night. Among the screams he heard cries of the fowls and other animals both wild and domestic which seemed to be thrown into confusion and greatly alarmed. He also became aware of a sulphurous odor that began to permeate the room.

Suddenly, the logs of the cabin where he was sleeping began to crack and twist, and the family with whom he had stayed began rushing to get their children out the door. William picked up the little three-year-old and held him tightly to his chest as he stumbled toward the door of the cabin.

Outside, there were people frantically running every which way, yet constantly stumbling and falling due to the earth being thrown into waves like the waves of the sea. For several minutes, chaos ensued until finally the worst seemed to be over. Though the quake occurred in the middle of the night, the darkness became abnormally severe and soon it was nearly impossible to see more than fifteen feet ahead. The darkness accompanied by the strong sulphurous odor and deafening noises was terrifying. Each member of the family made it out of the cabin and was huddled together on the ground in front of him crying and praying. William wrapped his arms around them and prayed along with them, doing his best to comfort them although his spirit was greatly troubled as well.

Morning was slow in coming with several lighter shocks occurring throughout the night. With daybreak came even more terror as a shock even more violent than the first shook the countryside. William watched as some of the cabins that had withstood the first shaking crumbled to the ground. The sound of cracking trees falling along with more terrified screams of both man and beast filled the air. William watched in horror as the earth began to split open only a few yards away. One man who was trying to get away could not outrun the fissure as it rapidly widened to some twenty feet and ultimately swallowed him up.

Finally, the latest shock began to die down and William noticed some of the militia that had camped out on the south side of the settlement began to assist the wounded. He began making his way to some of the nearby cabins searching for more injured. Amazingly, there were few people trapped in the rubble since it seemed that most of them had managed to get outside in the open. William worked tirelessly throughout the day helping to bind wounds and to comfort troubled hearts. Captain Ruddell informed them that the band of Creek Indians had disappeared—evidently frightened away by the earthquake. *It wasn't the Indian attack after all,* he thought to himself. *In reality the Lord was preparing me to minister to these affected by the quake.*

Over the course of the next week, William assisted the people of Little Prairie dig through the rubble and retrieve their belongings. Each day it seemed that the earth was in continual agitation although no violent shocks occurred like those of the first day. Several of the families had decided to leave the area, planning to settle with other loved ones as far from this place as they could get. All conversation centered around the earthquake. Some believed it was a judgment from God and others believed the world was coming to an end. Everyone was anxious to tell about their experiences during the ordeal.

Some of the most fantastic stories were those concerning the Mississippi River near by. At first the Great River seemed to recede from its banks with its waters gathering up like a mountain. Many of the boats that were on their way to New Orleans were left on bare sand due to the swiftness of the water's retreat. The poor sailors, watching the water rising up fifteen to twenty feet, escaped from the boats in a panic. Suddenly, the mountain of water expanded and the banks were overflowed with a tremendous torrent tearing many of the boats from their moorings and sending some as far as a quarter of a mile up little creeks that fed into the river. Most, however, were simply broken apart by the force of the water with their debris scattered across the river. Some even witnessed a great many fish left on the banks being unable to keep pace with the water. With all of the violent shocks, the banks were horribly torn and, in many places, the river totally rerouted. Small lakes formed where there had been none before and some that had existed prior to the quake totally disappeared. The most incredible account shared was that the river actually flowed backwards at one point!

William felt overwhelmed by it all, yet many were looking to him for encouragement and direction. He was searching for answers for himself, yet he was being called upon to explain why their whole lives were being turned upside down. He organized a prayer service among those who remained in the settlement of Little Prairie and was amazed at the response. Never had he ministered to more than a handful of the settlers here, yet there were more than fifty seeking souls present to lift their hearts up to heaven for help.

One gentleman was present who had been quite resistant to William's presence before. William greeted him warmly and was stirred when the man grasped his hand with both of his own and looked pleadingly into his eyes. There was a sense of desperation in the man that seemed to cry out with his whole being, "What is going to happen to me?"

William quieted the assembled seekers and thanked them for coming. "Many of you are looking for answers today…many of you, quite frankly, are asking God why," William began solemnly. "I wish that I had the answers but I don't. I would like to know when this nightmare will end but it goes beyond my limited understanding," he continued. "Yet this I do know," William stated more boldly while holding out his Bible, "we serve a God who is all-powerful and all-knowing. He knows the answers and He is able to calm the storm and calm those going through the storm! I may not always know the reason why, but I know my heavenly Father and He is trustworthy. He is able to give peace in the midst of the storm—a peace that passes all understanding. My friends, the Savior will help you today if you will allow Him. As we go to the Lord in prayer this morning I encourage you to humble yourself before a Holy God. I don't know if this is some type of judgment from Him or not, but I do know that our sin has separated us from Him and we are truly deserving of His judgment. Yet God loved us enough to send His only Son, Jesus Christ, to die on the cross for our sins. There is forgiveness available for you today and with that forgiveness there is hope. If you have never accepted Jesus Christ as your personal Lord and Savior then I encourage you to do that first thing this morning as we go to Him in prayer. Admit that you have sinned and confess those sins to Him this morning. Believe that Jesus died on the cross for you and commit your life to Him. Shall we pray together?" William said as he encouraged the people to stand. Several of those in attendance began to weep as the whole assembly began crying out to God.

After a time of corporate prayer William began ministering to people individually as most everyone lingered after the service. One by one he talked with them and opened the Bible with them—sharing words of comfort from the Scriptures.

CHAPTER 17
CHANCE ENCOUNTER

Camp Meeting at St. Michael, Spring 1812

As was common for the circuit rider, William was given a new circuit for a new year. He felt extremely blessed to be given the Cape Girardeau circuit, one that he had learned quite well riding with Jesse Walker a couple of years back. Although several miles north of the epicenter of the recent earthquake, Cape Girardeau was, nonetheless, impacted by the extraordinary act of nature. The last severe shock resulting from the earthquake was felt on February 7th, 1812 although small tremors continued at intervals until the present.

Even still, the number one topic of discussion among nearly all of those with whom William spoke was the shaking earth. His friend, Komoka, had hurried back to his village to check on his family after the first wave hit. The two of them had only a short time to visit the night before the quake, but they had at least swapped enough information to be able to keep in touch for the future. William had informed Komoka of the location near Cape Girardeau where his family had settled and had given him a rough idea of how often he ventured home for a visit.

Only last month Komoka had surprised him while he was heading home along "King's Highway" for that very purpose. A well placed shot from Komoka's sling had sufficiently startled William and Ol' Bess. Once he had calmed his horse the two enjoyed a good laugh. Komoka and William, who still carried a sling with him as well, enjoyed a contest of skill with their crude weapons. They reminisced about that day in the forest so many years ago and how one random meeting had stuck with them all this time. Komoka laughed as he shared of his boasting among his young Indian friends of this mighty weapon given him by a white warrior.

Much practicing had paid off for Komoka as he had impressed many Indian braves with his accuracy and skill. Of course he had also mastered the use of his bow and arrow, but it was this unusual gift from the white man that sparked more than a little discussion. William also shot his sling often although mostly when he was alone. More than once he had killed a squirrel or a rabbit with his crude weapon and cooked it over an open flame while out on the trail. It was for more than just enjoyment, however, that he maintained this practice. Although he carried a pistol with him, he hesitated firing it while in the wilderness; he preferred not to bring undue notice of his presence to any potential enemy.

Thomas Wright, one of the circuit riders who had been involved with the camp meeting near Cape Girardeau back in 1809, was now organizing a camp meeting at St. Michael. Now that William was riding the Cape Girardeau circuit, Thomas naturally asked William to assist him since St. Michael would potentially be an addition to his route. So, in April of 1812 the two made their way to the St. Michael settlement to make preparations. Thomas explained that St. Michael was founded as a Catholic settlement but he had sensed openness to a Methodist camp meeting on a recent trip through the area. Although the two had gotten acquainted a few years back, they had not really got to know each other until their heart-to-heart discussion on the trail that day. Thomas shared of his childhood years in Kentucky and then of his travels west of the Mississippi where, in 1803, he was converted. Like William, he had ultimately begun his labor for the Lord here in Missouri. Thomas felt like his calling was as a revivalist so he was striving to organize more camp meetings throughout the young Missouri Territory.

William, except for an occasional visit home when time permitted, had really not had anyone to talk openly with concerning personal struggles he was facing. Sure, Komoka was a good friend, but William's feelings about ministry, love, and the future were not topics of discussion that seemed appropriate when he was with his Indian brother. Thomas, however, had a very similar background, and most importantly, had accepted the same call of God as a circuit-riding preacher. Things that William had spent hours dwelling on while in the saddle now seemed to flow freely out of his heart as he talked with this dear Christian brother.

To his relief, Thomas admitted to having similar doubts and fears. Several of their colleagues had died young and were never married. Although he knew he was doing what the Lord wanted and was ready to die for his faith if that was how the Lord led, William shared how he still longed to find love and perhaps marry someday. His younger brother, John, was planning to marry a young girl from Cape Girardeau in the summer. William was now twenty-four years old. Would he ever find love? Would it be fair to marry only to spend so much time from home while riding his circuit? Would he be a circuit-riding preacher for the rest of his life? Was it a sin for him to think these thoughts and feel this way? The journey from Cape Girardeau to St. Michael seemed to take no time at all as the two rode and talked along the trail.

As with many settlements after the earthquake there was an openness to spiritual things that was not as prevalent before the life-changing event. Even before the camp site was completely cleared and prepared for use, there were frequent passersby expressing their excitement about the meetings. As word spread, families began arriving by wagon and on foot from several miles away.

At last the site was completed and Friday evening arrived with plenty of spiritually hungry and curious alike filing into the cleared area. Thomas took his place on the makeshift platform and welcomed the people. William circled the crowd praying to himself as well as keeping an eye open for any would-be troublemakers. He couldn't help his curiosity when it came to people. It was always interesting to study the different people that showed up for such events. There were those sincere believers who were simply hungry for a move of God. Others were those who were just curious and wanted to be where the action was. Unfortunately, there were all too often those who liked to cause trouble. Some even looked for opportunities to disrupt or to deceive.

He remembered well an event that happened when he was a boy back in Logan County, Kentucky, when Reverend McGready had dealt with an individual who presented himself as "God's prophet" and attempted to take over the meeting. He had loudly condemned the meeting as devil's work and boldly proclaimed himself as the only bearer of truth. Several in the meeting were charmed by his charismatic manner and speech, but William remembered how he felt a check in his spirit as the man spoke. Something within him, the Holy Spirit no doubt, seemed to alert him that this was not of God. He was greatly relieved when Reverend McGready along with a couple of strong farmers ushered the man from the premises and prevented him from reentering.

The service was well underway now with some songs being sung when William, who was still standing in the back observing the crowd, turned to make his way back towards the front of the gathering in order to prepare for his portion of the service. In his haste he failed to notice the young lady passing by at that moment and ran directly into her, causing her to stumble and drop her Bible.

William reached out and took her arm at the elbow to steady her. Apologizing profusely, he stooped down to pick up her Bible without letting go of her elbow. The young lady did not seem angry, but only stared wide-eyed at William without saying a word. After an awkward moment, she finally managed to accept the Bible and whisper a thank you before continuing on into the crowd.

What a lovely young lady, William thought to himself as he quickly made his way around the crowd to the platform.

CHAPTER 18
HANDSOME YOUNG MINISTER

St. Michael, Spring 1812 (Laura's Perspective)

News of the camp meeting at St. Michael reached the cabin on the Castor River late in the afternoon on the very day that the meetings were to begin. Laura had quietly gathered her things, tucked her Bible under her arm, and snuck out of the cabin. She knew that her father would not be happy when he found out where she was going. She was, however, nearly nineteen years old now and of late her independent spirit seemed to overpower her fear. It seemed ridiculous to her that her father was so negative about the church and the things of God.

On one particular day last fall, her dad seemed to be in good spirits so she attempted to talk with him about the only thing that was helping her cope with her grief and anger—the Lord Jesus Christ. Harrison flew into a rage condemning the church for its work among the Indians and for promoting peace and forgiveness. In his mind, turning to religion displayed weakness, and for him vengeance by force was the only way to deal with the red man! He strictly forbade her from participating in church activities as long as she was under his roof. Secretly Laura and her mother would read the Bible together and pray in her father's absence.

Of late, Laura had grown more defiant of her father's heavy yoke, and although she loved her father and prayed daily for his heart to soften towards God, she couldn't help but long for the day she could be free. She also dreamed of love—of finding someone with whom she could build a new home; a home where Christ's love would reign rather than hatred. She had seen what hatred can do to an individual and to a home, but she had also experienced the healing power of the Lord in her own life. It was not that she had forgotten what happened to her brother so many years ago, but she had actually come to a place in her spiritual walk where she could honestly pray for those who had done the evil deed. Would Jesus ask anything less of her than what He Himself demonstrated while on the cross, "Father forgive them for they know not what they do." She pondered these things in her heart as she quickly walked toward St. Michael.

She could hear the music before she saw the crowd and her heart seemed to quicken its pace slightly, as did her feet. How she had longed to sit under the preaching of God's Word and to worship Jesus with people of like faith. As she approached the meeting place and saw the people, she hesitated suddenly, first of all because of the surprising number of people that were present and second with a twinge of fear that someone might recognize her and report it to her father who would drag her from the meeting. The thought actually made her shiver. "I will not miss out on this opportunity, regardless of the consequences," she whispered aloud as she lowered her head down and pressed on into the crowd of people.

Suddenly, she felt the force of someone walking into her and fear gripped her at that instant—her father had already seen her and was going to make a scene! She felt herself falling backwards when a strong hand caught her elbow. She looked up and to her surprise, it was not her father, but a young man—a handsome young man with warm, friendly eyes. Her skin burned where he held her elbow and she seemed to lose her voice. The young man was excusing himself for his clumsiness as he reached down to pick up her Bible which she had dropped. Why was he still holding her elbow? Why was she feeling this way? Why couldn't she respond? There was one terrible moment of awkwardness when she knew she needed to say something but nothing seemed to come. His eyes were so kind.

"Thank you," she finally managed to whisper in a voice that was barely audible. With trembling hands she took the Bible from the gentleman and hurried on into the gathering of people. For several minutes, she was totally unaware of her surroundings. She didn't realize when one song had ended and another had begun. She didn't notice who was standing next to her or even what she herself was doing. She couldn't stop replaying the whole incident in her mind.

Why had she been so stupid! *All you had to do was say thank you and go on*, she thought to herself. *But oh, what a nice young man; I wonder if I will see him again*, she mused.

She finally got control of her thoughts and began to participate in the service. Although she did not know all of the words, she felt such joy as she sang out with the others in praise to God. Like a bird let out of a cage, her spirit felt freedom, released from prison, even if for only these few moments to sing and rejoice in the Lord among those of like belief. A minister took his place on the platform after the singing and began to lead in prayer.

She suddenly realized that this was the first time she had ever heard anyone pray other than her mother. Oh how her mother would enjoy this, her poor dear mother. She suddenly gasped so loudly that the woman next to her reached out and touched her hand asking if she was alright.

"Yes, excuse me…I am fine," she replied softly. She returned her gaze to the platform where stood the young man who had bumped into her only moments ago. He was a minister! He was the one bringing the message!

CHAPTER 19
UNEXPECTED DINNER GUEST

Second Day of Camp Meeting at St. Michael, 1812

Amazingly, Laura had been able to make it back home and into bed without her father ever knowing she had been gone. The next morning, Harrison ate a quick breakfast without saying a word to anyone before going out into the fields. Once he had left the house, Laura and her ma began talking about the camp meeting. Vera was taken back by her daughter's giddy demeanor as she began describing the young minister who had preached the night before. The usually reserved and mild-mannered daughter she was accustomed to suddenly transformed before her very eyes. She smiled to herself as Laura replayed the evening for her in great detail. She had known this day would come but dreaded it in some ways. Oh, not that she did not wish her daughter every happiness but the thought of losing her closest friend saddened her. Loneliness crept over her thinking about the day that her daughter would leave and only she and Harrison would remain at the little cabin on Castor River. She realized that it may not happen soon but this was surely the first time her daughter had spoken of a man in this manner. *Did the young man feel the same about her?* Vera wondered.

The two worked out a plan for Laura to attend the camp meeting again that day. Vera put together a list of items that were needed at the cabin and resolved to appease Harrison if he showed any animosity to Laura making a trip to town for supplies. She kissed her daughter on the cheek and sent her on her way. "Lord, direct Laura and may she find happiness," she prayed quietly as a tear ran down her cheek.

Laura arrived in St. Michael to a torrent of activity, people were everywhere! She didn't believe she had ever seen so much activity in the young community. She decided to go by the Bernbaum's store first and pick up the things on her list, feeling it best to have the items in hand in case her father showed up.

"Good morning to you Miss Laura!" Mr. Bernbaum bubbled as Laura entered the mercantile. He offered his large hand which still swallowed hers even though she was grown. She still couldn't help but giggle when she saw the merchant for he was so jovial and full of life.

Laura handed him the list and made her way to the books as was her normal routine on those rare occasions when she was allowed to come to town for supplies. It didn't take her long to be carried away on another romantic adventure as she picked up where she had left off in her favorite book.

A tap on her shoulder brought her back to reality. "Laura, we have something that we would like to ask you," Mrs. Bernbaum said sweetly. Laura had only met Mrs. Bernbaum a few times over the years but she was without a doubt the sweetest lady alive—at least that was Laura's opinion. "Laura," Mrs. Bernbaum continued, "we noticed that you attended the service last night and were wondering if you would like to have lunch with us today, that is if you will be staying in town for the service?"

Laura was thrilled at the invitation. She could count on one hand how many times she had eaten somewhere other than her own home. "Yes, I would be pleased to accept your invitation," Laura said with a big smile. "Thank you so very much for thinking of me," she added.

Mrs. Bernbaum seemed sincerely pleased by her acceptance of the invitation and instructed her to arrive at their house, which was right next to the mercantile, at noon. Mr. Bernbaum offered to keep Laura's order over in the corner of the store since she would be back later but Laura chose to keep it in hand. Laura graciously thanked the Bernbaums again before stepping back out into the sunshine.

It was a lovely spring day and Laura soaked up the sun's rays and took a deep breath of satisfaction before making her way to the camp meeting site. Not knowing for sure when the morning service would begin, she hoped to find a place a little closer to the front than the night before. She winced slightly as she realized that her motivation was more to have a better look at the young minister than for spiritual reasons. Lost in her thoughts, she turned the corner towards the camp site. Some yelling and cheering brought her head up and drew her attention to a small crowd gathered in a circle out behind the meeting area. Her curiosity effectively piqued, she made her way over to the crowd and her mouth dropped at the sight of the young minister, and wrestling of all things!

She tapped the nearest spectator on the shoulder and asked, "Why are they fighting?"

"Oh, they are not really fighting; this is just a friendly wrestling competition," came the reply, but the man never took his eyes from the action. "The young minister has yet to be beat!" he concluded with excitement.

"Excuse me for bothering you, but doesn't the minister have to preach here in a few minutes?" Laura ventured.

The spectator, still keeping his eyes on the wrestling match replied, "He said that another preacher is bringing the message this morning so he wanted to get in on the action."

Laura, still in a slight state of shock, turned her attention to the wrestling match in progress. The young minister must be giving up nearly twenty pounds to his opponent and a good three or four inches in height, but he seemed to be holding his own. Wrestling was a common form of entertainment among young men for her father had often mentioned such events, but she wasn't sure if she had ever known of a minister taking part. She smiled slightly as the young minister successfully pinned his opponent with much jubilation from the excited onlookers.

The young minister raised his hand to speak, "Thank you all, but I'm afraid that I have obligations that await me and must improve my appearance or else I may not be allowed to participate."

The crowd began to boo, mostly in fun, although it was obvious that a couple of other challengers were eager to have their opportunity with the reigning champion. Laura stayed and watched a couple of other matches before walking over to the camp meeting where people were starting to gather. Although not as well attended as the night before, the morning service hosted a decent crowd and a powerful message was provided from a minister by the name of Wright. Laura also learned that the young minister's name was William Travers for he led the prayer time for the morning service. She was unsure how she missed the name the night before, but she was quite sure she would never forget it from this day forward.

The morning service went a little past noon, but Mr. Bernbaum was in attendance so Laura was in no hurry. No doubt Mrs. Bernbaum had skipped the service to prepare the meal.

"What a treat," Laura thought to herself as she made her way to the Bernbaum's home for the noon meal. It was not just the meal that she anticipated, but also the Christian fellowship. Oh how she had longed for that! She knocked on the door of the home next to the mercantile as instructed by her host earlier that day.

Mrs. Bernbaum opened the door and squealed with delight as she welcomed Laura into the room. "I am so pleased that you could come," Mrs. Bernbaum bubbled as she put her arm around Laura directing her to a seat at the table. "You are the first to arrive but the others will be along shortly," Mrs. Bernbaum said as she hurried back into the kitchen area.

Laura looked around at the table and place settings, it was beautiful! The plates and cups were embellished with beautiful flower designs and real silverware was placed next to them. Laura picked up each item inspecting it closely with pure admiration. "Others will be along shortly" Mrs. Bernbaum had said. It suddenly donned on her that there were four place settings at the table. *Who else would be joining them for lunch?* she wondered.

She heard voices in conversation outside the house before the door opened and Mr. Bernbaum's unmistakable voice reverberated throughout the dwelling.

"Come on in, son, and make yourself at home," Mr. Bernbaum said. "It's an honor to have you join us for lunch today. I'm very sorry that Reverend Wright was unable to join us as well," Mr. Bernbaum continued as he and his companion appeared in the doorway to the dining area.

Laura felt like her heart was up in her throat and she could hardly breathe. Standing before her was William Travers! And he was joining them for lunch!

"Laura, I see you beat us here," Mr. Bernbaum said with a smile. "Have you met Reverend William Travers?"

Laura stood to her feet and held out her hand. "Yes, we've run into each other," she said shyly but with a slight grin forming on her lips.

William laughed as he took her hand, "quite literally I'm afraid," he added. "I ran right into her last night during the meeting and nearly knocked her down," William continued as he took his seat.

William, Laura and Mr. Bernbaum chatted as Mrs. Bernbaum finished setting the table. Laura, although quite anxious at first, began to relax and thoroughly enjoy the wonderful meal and pleasant conversation. William seemed so down to earth and was extremely easy to talk to.

For a short time, Laura forgot all about her difficulties with her father and the worries of tomorrow. It was as if the whole world had stopped spinning and all that existed or mattered was what she was experiencing right at that moment.

CHAPTER 20
WAR

Missouri Territory, Summer 1812

The camp meeting at St. Michael had been successful and, as a result, the preaching points along William's circuit were increased by one. Not only was William thrilled to have more hungry souls to whom he could minister, but he was pleased by the prospect of seeing the lovely Laura every four to five weeks. How sweet she had been as they chatted during lunch at the Bernbaum home. Had she known that he would be there? Had the Bernbaums intended for them to meet—or was it providence? His thoughts seemed to never stray too far from that afternoon conversation as the fresh spring breezes slowly gave way to the stifling summer heat.

John, William's younger brother, was married on a hot mid-summer's afternoon on the banks of the Whitewater River near the family home. John and his father had been slowly but steadily working on a cabin for him and his new bride over the course of the last few months. William lent a hand every chance he got when in between circuit rides and now the simple but functional habitation was ready to receive its excited homesteaders. Jacob and Sarah had given John and Mary, the lovely bride, ten acres of ground adjoining theirs but that was not all that the young couple received. Among their wedding gifts were many essentials that newlyweds need as they begin their new life together: a bushel of potatoes, a few gallons of corn meal, a slab of cured meat, and several combs of honey.

Although William was happy for his brother and new sister-in-law there was a heaviness in him that he couldn't seem to shake no matter how hard he tried. He finally slipped away from the celebration and made his way downstream to a shallow pool. Sitting down on the bank, he began skipping rocks across the water.

Sarah had sensed her son's inner struggle as well. Noticing his exit, she made her way to William's side. She slipped her shoes off and sat down next to him, letting her feet dangle in the water. "I bet I know what you're thinking," she said as she playfully elbowed him in the side. "Will it ever be me?" she continued as she turned her face to look at William.

William skipped another rock before answering. "I can't believe I'm feeling this way on the day of my own brother's wedding. I'm just being selfish I guess. I do want to marry someday, but I also have this fear that somehow I might be dishonoring God in doing so," William said with pleading eyes as he turned to face his mother.

"It's natural for you to want to marry, don't you know that God gives us that desire?" Sarah replied, putting her hand on his. "I've prayed for years that God would use you *and* that he would provide you with a wonderful helpmate someday," she continued. "I know you're worried about marrying someone and then leaving them alone for weeks at a time. I also understand that you feel called to be a circuit-riding preacher right now and you don't want to do anything contrary to God's will," Sarah said as she put an arm around William's shoulder and pulled him in close. "Don't you know by now that God is big enough to work this out? God will send you a wife when the time is right," she concluded, kissing him on the cheek.

Early the next morning, William saddled up Ol' Bess and made his way into Cape Girardeau to visit Elder Parker. He smiled as he recalled the conversation the evening before with his ma.

"She always seems to know just what to say," he whispered. Bess pricked her ears at his voice. "It's alright ol' girl...I'm just talking to myself again," he chuckled at himself. "That's what happens when you spend too many hours on the trail alone," he said, patting the horse's neck as they were just reaching the outskirts of the town.

Cape Girardeau was bustling as usual but there seemed to be tension in the air. He picked up the pace as he neared the house where Elder

Parker stayed when he was in town; his curiosity mounting with each step of the horse.

His first knock brought an instant response as the door opened almost immediately.

"Oh William, please come in," Elder Parker said as he motioned for William to enter. "I was actually getting ready to head over to the town square to learn more about the war," he explained.

"War? This is the first I've heard of it," William exclaimed with sincere surprise.

"Oh forgive me William, I'm afraid that I am a little rattled at the moment," Elder Parker said. "Why don't you come along with me and I'll share what I know as we walk," he continued, placing his hat on his head and heading out the door. "I've only received scattered reports so far, but it seems that President Madison has declared war on the British.[9] As a matter of fact, I understand that it was actually back in June that the formal declaration was made, but it is just recently that we received appeals for recruits to join a militia that is forming in Illinois. I've heard reports that the British, with their ongoing tension with France, have been boarding American ships under the suspicion that we are transporting goods to their enemy. Evidently, some of our sailors have even been kidnapped and are being forced to serve in the British navy! There have been ongoing tensions as well with the British presence in Canada and their supposed support of Tecumseh, who has pledged to drive the Americans out of the frontier," Elder Parker continued as they made their way to the court square.

"Tecumseh, I've heard of him," William interjected. "He's the Shawnee Indian leader that made that journey down the Mississippi River last year trying to unite more tribes to his cause," William added.

"There's a rumor that Tecumseh predicted the earthquake last December and since it's occurrence more tribes have conceded to join him since they believe him to have some power," Elder Parker stated with a sigh.

William stopped suddenly with a look of amazement on his face.

"What is it son?" Elder Parker said while putting a hand on William's shoulder.

---

9. Historical Note: This was the beginning of the War of 1812.

"The earthquake…you see I was in Little Prairie when the first shock hit," William began. "It probably sounds amazing, but the earthquake very likely saved my life and only God knows how many others," William paused as he wiped the sweat from his brow. "You see, my Indian friend Komoka, a Delaware Indian that I met as a boy, had warned us of an imminent attack by a party of Creek warriors and we had confirmed their presence just south of Little Prairie," William continued. "That very night the earthquake hit and scared them away. It just struck me that the very event that Tecumseh may be using to promote his hatred toward the Americans is the very thing that kept me and the people of Little Prairie from that attack."

"It is quite extraordinary that something as terrible as this earthquake could both serve to protect you and the folks at Little Prairie, as well as be used as a vice to influence others to do such evil," Elder Parker said, shaking his head.

The two continued their walk to the court square where several men were gathered.

A well-dressed young man was addressing the crowd with great animation and passion. "Are we going to stand idly by while our American brothers and sisters are being attacked and brutally killed at the hands of such savagery? I say 'no sir' and I implore you to join with me. Take up your arms and let us join with the Illinois militia to force these oppressive and divisive British brigands out of our lands and bring the villainy of Tecumseh and his band of murdering savages to an end!"

Some cheers were going up while others just looked on. For some, the war seemed far away with little risk of affecting their everyday lives here west of the Mississippi. For others, their sense of patriotism was heightened and the thought of the British once more threatening their freedom served to move them into action. For others still, the tactics of Tecumseh, no doubt mingled with their past entanglements with warring Indians, was enough to prepare their hearts for battle.

William watched as several men raised their hands to commit to joining the eloquent speaker on his journey to Illinois.

CHAPTER 21
HYDROPHOBIA

Missouri Territory, Late Summer 1812

Along with bringing the good news of the gospel throughout the territory, the circuit rider was often also a bearer of general information. Whether at a settlement or in a solitary cabin in the wilderness, there was always a hunger for the latest news from the outside world. This particular trip for William served, in many ways, as more of a war announcement expedition than it did a ministry opportunity. With growing frustration, William answered the curious and concerned, leaving little time for ministry of the Word. It was not that William himself was unconcerned about the young country's situation, but it was always amazing to him how things of this world always had a way of superseding the things of God. Was it not the hand of Providence that directed the affairs of men? Did not God intervene in the events of the Revolutionary War and clearly influence the formation of this young country called America? If people would only look to Him in all circumstances—especially during times of trial. For many, however, all that mattered was the moment and, more specifically, how that moment affected them.

"Oh God," William prayed as he made his way to the next stop on his route, "Open our eyes that we may see what is most important. May your message of forgiveness and salvation become so real to all who hear it. Yes, guide our leaders and protect our soldiers, may Your will be done and those who would do us harm be thwarted. But most of all, heavenly Father, may the message of Your love go forth with great effectiveness. May Your kingdom come on earth as it is in heaven!"

William awoke early the next morning and began his 4:00 a.m. prayer as normal. Since the camp meeting in St. Michael, he had begun lifting Laura's name to heaven during his prayer time, but only since the talk with his mother had he finally been able to completely surrender the matter to the Lord. Even now there was a peace that seemed to cover him as he once again submitted his future to the Lord's guidance.

He was now more than halfway through his route which should bring him into St. Michael in a couple of days. The thought of seeing Laura again made him smile as he mounted Ol' Bess and started on down the trail. Many hours in the saddle lent itself to a lot of thinking and studying. William strived to utilize the time as wisely as possible by reading his Bible or other books, but he also liked to just think about things. Lately, Laura had been a frequent subject of contemplation but he also spent time studying on how he might become a more effective minister.

This trip especially seemed to foster within him a greater desire to educate the flock that was in his care. The frustration that he had especially felt this time around was due to the lack of hunger for God's Word on his listener's part; or even a semblance of recognition to its importance to their lives. Much of it, no doubt, was due to the amount of illiteracy that was prevalent. He thought back to how his mother had spent time with him and John each day teaching them how to read and to do arithmetic. Several of the homes he visited lacked even one parent who was able to read. If more people were able to read then they could read the Bible themselves rather than waiting sometimes up to six weeks for the circuit rider to pass that way again.

William thought about his Uncle Zeb and how he peddled books. "I wonder," William said aloud. "Perhaps if I could get my hands on some primers with the basics in them," he continued talking to himself as he rode along. Even if he could get some copies into the hands of those who could read then at least they would have a tool to help them educate their children.

Furthermore, the general ignorance that he witnessed alarmed him. If he could provide an occasional book that would educate and inform no doubt it would be a blessing. Wasn't part of his ministry to also meet man's physical and mental needs, along with the spiritual?

One home he had visited just a few days back was a frightening example of such ignorance. As he was riding onto the homestead, he had heard wailing and crying. Fearing that death had come to the cabin he began immediately preparing himself mentally for what would be required of him. Upon arriving at the cabin he dismounted and called out to the house. The distraught young mother ran out to meet him, but was having difficulty even calming down enough to speak. Having visited the family on a number of occasions, William was known by the young lady and was able to settle her down after gently comforting her. Much to his surprise the young mother did not lose a loved one but was only convinced that she would do so in the very near future. It seemed that a bird had lit on a window sill just moments before his arrival. In her mind this indicated that death would soon come to the family. The best William could figure was that sometime in the young lady's past there had been a death in her family and, by chance, a bird had lit on their window sill at the time of passing. In her reasoning, the bird in the window had caused the death, rather than being a mere coincidence. William was unable to convince her that her superstition was unfounded, but prayed with her nonetheless, which seemed to bring the frightened young lady some comfort.

Of course, this was not the only incident of this sort that William had experienced. He had long heard folks say that the first thunder of early spring awakened all snakes from their long winter slumber. One elderly man down around New Madrid had told him that the sighting of a white mule at the start of a journey was a signal of bad luck.

William admitted to himself that he had much to learn as well since he had no formal education—even about the Bible. It was to his advantage that he loved to read and he spent many hours doing just that. He also seemed to have a good memory and could remember still many of the sermons he had heard as a boy under the ministry of Reverend McGready. It was not uncommon for him to borrow a book from Elder Parker or another circuit-rider friend to devour during the hours on the trail.

Yes, this was a good idea, he thought to himself. "I'm going to speak with Elder Parker about this and see if I can begin transporting some books to sell or give away, even if it means bringing along a pack mule," he concluded out loud while rubbing Ol' Bess' ears.

William was making his way along the St. Francis River when a sudden shot rang out from about a half mile away. Bess' ears turned and she stiffened. William removed the pistol from his pack and checked the load. For a few moments he sat still, waiting for the sound of other shots or for the racing of hooves. Finally, he gave Bess a kick and started her in the direction of the shot. He was wary, but if someone was in danger or hurt he felt like he should help.

William could hear the sound of growling, slightly at first but growing louder the closer he got. Suddenly he heard a yell, "Mister, hey mister!" His eyes followed the sound of the voice to find a young boy up in an oak tree about seventy yards away. At the base of the tree was a wild dog which seemed intent upon getting to the boy. William kicked Bess and ran her toward the dog with himself yelling and whistling along the way. The dog backed off several yards but was not, however, deterred from its original mission. A flash of fear gripped William as he realized that the dog may have hydrophobia. He aimed his pistol at the animal and fired but missed. Again the dog backed off but did not run away. He directed Bess closer to the tree to retrieve the boy. The large, wild-eyed dog began moving towards him and it looked as if it might attack.

There was no time to reload so almost without thinking William pulled the sling from his pack along with one of the stones that he kept along with it. He swiftly swung the sling and let loose just as the dog began to lunge forward. The rock hit the dog squarely in the head, jarring the animal and rendering it momentarily confused and alarmed. William swiftly moved Bess under the oak tree, allowing the young boy to jump down behind him. They took off at a run with the boy pointing the way to his home. In a matter of moments they met the boy's father, who had evidently heard the unfamiliar pistol shot and was running through the woods with a rifle.

William cried out, "There's a wild dog behind us…maybe hydrophobia!"

Almost immediately the man's eyes focused behind them as they rode by and they heard the shot before William slowed the horse and turned. The boy jumped from Bess and ran to his pa who was standing over the fallen dog.

"Don't get too close son...see the foam around his mouth. That there dog is mighty sick and he would make you terrible sick as well," the man said as he pulled the boy to himself.

William dismounted and joined the two near the dog.

The boy excitedly told his pa the story of how he had shot a squirrel and was retrieving it when this dog appeared. He had at first called to the dog, thinking it might be friendly, but when the dog began running at him growling he had dropped his rifle and climbed up the nearest tree.

"Then this here fella came along and shot at the dog with his pistol but missed," the boy continued excitedly. "The dog was getting ready to rush him when he shot him with some kind of sling and a rock. The dog was stunned some so I jumped on the horse and we took off like a shot," he concluded.

"I'm beholdin' to you mister," the man said, extending his hand to William. "we'd be pleased if you would join us at the house for a bite to eat."

William accompanied the family to their home just over the next ridge where the boy's worried mother was waiting impatiently. With the unknown shot and their boy alone in the woods, they had thought the worst. Although initially relieved to see her son safe, the young mother again became upset as the boy retold his harrowing tale about the wild dog which somehow had grown bigger and meaner at the retelling. The mother embraced her son and then took William's hand.

"Words cannot express how truly grateful I am that you came along when you did...and that you were willing to help," she said with tears streaming down her face. "You will be our honored guest for supper," she exclaimed while wiping her eyes. "James, you go and keep our guest company while I fix up something to eat," she told her son.

James was eager to please as he led William back outside to introduce him to their horse and show him around. The boy's pa, Edward Tidwell, took a shovel and made his way out to bury the dog; the risk being too great to leave the animal exposed even a short while for fear that other animals could be infected.

William spent the afternoon with the kind family and immensely enjoyed their company. The Tidwells were originally from Tennessee and had only settled here near the St. Francis River about a year back. James was their only son for they had lost their daughter to scarlet fever back in '08. The family had been exposed to the gospel in Tennessee but had never been baptized. Much to William's delight, Edward asked that he baptize them all in the St. Francis River before leaving. William opened the Scriptures with them and explained more fully the meaning of baptism and asked them if they had each accepted Jesus Christ into their heart as Lord and Savior. A tear made its way down Edward's cheek as he bowed his head and prayed.

A circling hawk was the only witness, other than God and the angels, as Edward and his family were raised out of the water with their hands in the air in praise to the Lord. It was truly a day worth remembering—not only for this fine family but for William as well. His heart was so filled with joy that he felt like it might explode with thanksgiving to God for this divine appointment He had provided. An open invitation was extended, more like an order really, that William was to lodge with them any time he passed through this way again. He promised that he would as he mounted up and prepared to leave.

"Wait just a minute," Mrs. Tidwell told William as she ran into the cabin. She came out carrying three ears of corn and some jerked beef and handed them to William. "It's not much but it is just our way of saying thanks to our sling shot circuit-riding preacher," she said with a big smile.

Sling Shot Circuit Rider, William thought to himself as he was riding away. *Now that is a new one!* he laughed out loud as he turned his horse north along the St. Francis River.

William rode into St. Michael just before noon two days later and was greeted warmly by Mr. Bernbaum at the mercantile. Word was spread that he was in town and a handful of people gathered for a service. More than a little disappointed, William realized that Laura was not among the group. He brought a message out of Ephesians chapter two and remained after to talk with the attendees.

Finally he worked up his courage to inquire about Laura. Mr. Bernbaum frowned slightly before answering. "William, that there young lady is in a rough spot...she surely is," he began. "Such a fine young lady and I don't know when I've ever seen her happier than the day we all had lunch together," he continued with his gaze drifting off as he remembered. "You see, her father is a very angry and bitter man and, unfortunately for Laura and her ma, he all too often takes it out on them. Some years back, before the Mrs. and I were here, Laura's brother was killed in an Indian attack. Laura's father, Harrison Smith is his name; he just couldn't handle it I guess. They say he was already prone to it, but he has venom in him now…towards the Indians mostly but also to anyone who he feels supports them. He feels that preachers and the church in general are his enemies too. I guess it is because many Christians recognize that the Indians are made in God's image and seek to evangelize them—at least those that are willing to hear," Mr. Bernbaum continued. He looked solemnly at William, "Son, when Harrison found out that Laura had snuck out of the house to attend the camp meeting he was furious. The very evening of our lunch together she was beaten by her father and is no longer allowed to even come into town. At least that's the word that has gotten back to us. Mrs. Bernbaum ventured out that way a couple weeks after the meeting but was turned back by Harrison; she wasn't even allowed to see the womenfolk." William felt the anger rising within him along with the shock of this news.

"Can you tell me where they live?" William asked, not being able to disguise his anger.

"William," Mr. Bernbaum pleaded, "it might not be the best thing to ride out there. He's a very hard man and almost impossible to reason with."

However, William was undeterred and insistent, and so he was given directions to the Smith homestead along the Castor River.

William prayed to himself as he rode north along the river. He desperately attempted to bring his anger in check for he knew that it would only hinder his efforts if he lost his temper. But the thought of anyone hurting Laura made his blood boil and caused his fists to clinch.

He rode up over a ridge and saw below him the cabin that Mr. Bernbaum had described to him. Scanning the area carefully, he slowly walked the horse down the ridge to the front of the cabin. "Hello the house," he yelled out as he drew near the front door.

Laura stepped to the door and with an excited grin on her face began walking towards him.

William dismounted and started toward Laura when suddenly she stopped, staring over his shoulder. She slowly lowered her head and William felt a chill run down his spine as a hand gripped his shoulder.

"Who are you and what do you want here?" a stern voice boomed in his ear.

William turned slowly to face the man whom he could only assume was Harrison. The man's eyes were hard and his stare disturbing. William's first thought was that this man must be miserable inside. He was surprised that his initial emotional reaction to the man before him was actually pity.

"I said, who are you?" Harrison repeated.

"My name is William Travers, sir, and I am a Methodist minister," William replied. "I was in hopes that I could offer my services to you and your family," William continued boldly but respectfully.

"A preacher are you?" Harrison growled. "We'll not be needing the likes of you 'round here. You can just mount that mare of yours and head on down the trail," Harrison said gruffly.

William put his foot in the stirrup and stepped up into the saddle. "Sir, I honestly desire to help you…I understand that you have experienced a tremendous loss and I know in my heart that God is able to minister to you and heal your hurt," William shared sincerely.

Harrison's reaction was immediate; he slapped the horse's rump and cursed loudly causing Bess to jump and buck. William grabbed a hold of the pommel with one hand and the reins with the other and desperately attempted to gain control of Bess. Bess was already over the ridge and out of site of the cabin before William was able to calm her down.

"Oh Lord, please help Laura and give me wisdom to know what to do," William prayed as he headed Bess back towards St. Michael.

CHAPTER 22
LOVE LETTER

Missouri Territory, Fall of 1812

Elder Parker was favorable to William's idea of distributing books along his circuit, but funds were limited. William's folks donated some money towards the cause as did some of the faithful from his home church. Although he didn't have the number of books he had hoped for, he was pleased that it was at least a start. Rather than money, some people actually donated books. One particular book was of great interest to William—a medical book donated by the local physician. He had recently acquired a more up-to-date copy and graciously offered it to William either to sell for cash or to use as he saw fit. Although William had no desire to become a practicing doctor he, nonetheless, saw the great need for basic medical knowledge throughout the territory. Not only was William called upon for spiritual matters and news information but was occasionally asked to offer advice on illnesses; something of which he knew next to nothing about. William had all too often seen an illness steal the life of a child with the family looking to him for answers. As much as he enjoyed reading and with plenty of time on the trail to do so, he felt confident that he could at least gain some basic knowledge by reading the medical book.

While in Cape Girardeau he received little news concerning the war, although he was informed of some other men who had left to join the militia. Some locally scattered Indian attacks were reported, but the majority of the fighting was taking place much further north and east. A man by the name of Henry Dodge from Ste. Genevieve was appointed as a general in the local militia that was formed to protect the Missouri Territory against Indian attack. No doubt the growing tension due to the

Indian attacks was why he had not seen Komoka for a while. Some of the settlers had itchy trigger fingers due to the heightened fears and were not likely to ask whether he was a friendly Delaware or an angry Creek.

William began his regular route with greater enthusiasm in that he felt excited to be able to offer Bibles and primers to these families with whom he had come to know and love. Upon hitting the trail, he immediately tore into the medical book and began reading about setting broken bones and making splints, as well as treating other diverse illnesses.

He was so caught up in reading the medical book that he nearly rode right past his first preaching point. After the message he presented the Bibles and other resources that he brought along and was pleased at the interest that was displayed for the literature. Although he had not required it, some paid him a little bit for the Bibles. Of course, money was somewhat hard to come by so many bartered for what they bought. He remembered that his pa had accepted some unusual payments back in Kentucky for the shoes he sold. There was one man who actually paid him in coon skins!

The circuit rider's salary was about $80 per year, although William rarely ever received that much compensation. Thankfully, he lived close enough to his folks who were always willing to help him out if he had need of something. He had learned, however, that to decline an offer of payment was offensive to some. Call it pride, perhaps, but they wouldn't take something for free. William couldn't help but respect that attitude since he had run into plenty of other individuals who felt like everyone owed them something. Although the literature was primarily meant to be a blessing to his flock, it also helped him earn a little extra money; for this he was very thankful.

Overall the literature was well received so that when William arrived at St. Michael he had only three Bibles left and one primer. His heart was heavy when he dismounted at Bernbaum's mercantile. He paused briefly, staring at the house next door before entering the store. It had been nearly six months since he and Laura had eaten lunch together at the Bernbaum's house, and around three months now since his attempt at talking with Harrison. He had considered trying again but felt in his spirit that the time was not yet right. His feelings for Laura remained unchanged and, although difficult at times, he was continuing to commit the situation to the Lord. As usual Mr. Bernbaum lifted his spirits with his usual chipper demeanor and friendly smile. He ended up having lunch with the Bernbaums and the talk came around to Laura.

Laura's mother, Vera, had been into the store a few weeks back and seemed concerned about her daughter. Laura had become withdrawn and rarely talked even to her. Harrison had found out that Laura was infatuated with William and had threatened to harm him if ever he set foot on the place again. Vera had encouraged the Bernbaums to warn William to be careful when in or around St. Michael because she believed that Harrison meant him harm. Mrs. Bernbaum added that Harrison had a couple of friends from Mine La Motte with whom he drank from time to time and rumor had it that they were "going to teach that circuit rider a thing or two when they got him alone."

She pleaded with William to stay away for a spell in fear for his safety.

"No," William replied resolutely, "I will not be buffaloed by those who would fight against God, and as long as I am in the center of the Lord's will then that is exactly who they will be fighting against. It is Laura and her state of mind that concerns me right now," William continued.

"Let's agree together in prayer for her that she will hold on to hope and that our heavenly Father will minister to her heart even now."

The three joined hands and spent several minutes in prayer for Laura and her family. During the prayer, William felt an increasing burden to write Laura a letter.

At the conclusion of the prayer time, William mentioned this idea and Mrs. Bernbaum agreed to attempt the delivery of it. Mr. Bernbaum supplied William with pen and paper and the couple busied themselves with little tasks around the house while William wrote:

Laura,
I take pen in hand to share with you all that is in my heart. I have been made aware of the situation you endure at home with your father, who is himself in inner turmoil and in desperate need of the Savior's touch. I cannot begin to imagine the loneliness and hurt that you have experienced, but can say with the utmost assurance that our heavenly Father sees

all and is fully capable of ministering to you in your time of deepest need. I pray for you daily and earnestly believe that God will bring you peace and victory. And now, if I could be so bold, I would like to share with you something that has been growing in my heart since the first moment that we met. Although we barely know each other and we have only been able to talk on a couple of occasions, there has not been a day go by that I do not think of you. Each time I pray for you there is a growing sense of certainty that I believe to be from the Holy Spirit, in the belief that God has ordained for us to be together. Please forgive my boldness but I feel impressed to share openly with you my feelings since I know you to be downcast and suffering in spirit at this time. If I could just relay to you that not only can you trust in our heavenly Father, but you can also trust in me, for I too love you. Please be patient in your endurance of difficulty and trust that God will work all out for the best.
Sincerely,
William

Upon completing the letter, William prayed silently over it that it would reach its intended destination and truly be a blessing to Laura in her hour of need. He stood and handed the letter to Mrs. Bernbaum, who once again assured him that she would do all that was in her power to make sure Laura received it. William then thanked the Bernbaums for the meal and especially their friendship and assistance before taking his leave.

He spent the remainder of the afternoon visiting different homes and families in and around St. Michael. As he had expected, he left St. Michael that evening having distributed the remainder of his literature.

"That's a relief for you I guess, hey Ol' Bess?" he laughed as he patted the horse on the neck "The load is lighter from here on out," he quipped as the two made their way out of St. Michael on the trail east.

CHAPTER 23
HOPELESSNESS

Cabin on Castor River, Fall of 1812

Laura sat under her favorite oak tree on the family farm staring up at the stars. The night air was crisp and the skies so clear that it seemed the stars were almost within arms reach. A little gust of wind gave her a chill so she pulled her shawl up tighter over her shoulders. It was hard for her to pray—to even feel.

"God where are you?" she sighed. "Do I even have a future?" she said as she lowered her head and wiped a solitary tear from her cheek.

She had been so happy the day she had spent in St. Michael during the camp meeting in April. It was more than just happiness for her; it had given her hope. There was more out there than what she was experiencing; there was more to life! The feelings she had while talking with the young minister were something special, so very real. She had not been so lucky sneaking back into the house that second evening, and her father was quick to condemn her actions. More than that he had struck her; but the physical pain was nothing compared to the emotional blow.

Her father had been angry often and she had feared him at times, but he had never hit her as he did that night. It seemed to drain all of the life out of her. As the months had gone by she felt more and more hopeless. It was as if she was a prisoner in her own home. She was no longer allowed to go to town by herself or even accompany her parents when they made the trip.

Somehow Pa had found out about her lunch with the minister and had confronted her about it. It was not in her to lie so she freely admitted it as well as indicated that she had feelings for the man. Harrison stormed out

104

of the room and refused to even speak with her for several days. When at last he did speak, it was merely to warn her; she was not to have any further contact with the minister and he would make sure that this trouble-maker would get the message to stay away from her as well. It was more than Laura could bear so she had retreated into a shell where she seldom spoke or even exhibited a semblance of existence. She knew her mother was worried but she simply didn't care; she couldn't find it within herself to care about anything anymore.

"Oh God...just let me die," she whispered again, gazing into the heavens. "I simply have no desire to go on."

CHAPTER 24
GOOD SAMARITAN

Near Cape Girardeau, December 1812

A light sprinkling of snow lay on the forest floor with fresh rabbit tracks across the path in front of him. Bess plodded on effortlessly along the route that had now become routine. William felt confident that Ol' Bess could do it blindfolded. William had left at sunup in order to get an early start on his circuit. His restlessness had not subsided despite spending a couple of days with his family along the Whitewater River. He simply couldn't get Laura off of his mind. She was never far from his thoughts, but over the last couple of weeks there was an unsettled feeling that rankled him. If she was truly as discouraged as was described to him then what might she do? Of even greater concern, what might Harrison do in response? William had made a decision the night before to confront Harrison again. He prayed earnestly much of the evening and was praying continuously in the saddle that day.

"God please prepare the way for me…make a way where there seems to be no way," he prayed. "Lord, you love Laura and you love her father. You are all powerful and I know that You are able to intervene in this situation."

Although he rarely cried, he felt so overcome with emotion that the tears began to flow. "Look at me, Bess, I'm a horrible mess!" he exclaimed wiping his eyes with his sleeve.

William was no more than five hours out of Cape Girardeau when he noticed some unusual tracks crossing the trail in front of him. The tracks were those of a horse, but they were sporadic, as if the animal had been spooked or injured, maybe both. Suddenly William realized that he had failed to load his pistol as he normally did upon hitting the trail. He quickly pulled out his powder horn and began to ready his pistol while keeping his eyes and ears open for any movement or unnatural sounds.

By the time his pistol was ready, he had decided to follow the tracks. His gut feeling was that the horse's rider may be injured. An injured man in this weather could get hypothermia quickly so he nudged Bess on and began following the tracks. Within three hundred yards or so, the tracks indicated that the horse had slowed to a walk. William lifted his gaze to scan the wooded area in which he found himself.

Finally, his eye caught something unnatural in the present setting. Where everything should be vertical, such as the trees, he detected something horizontal. He leaned over in the saddle to get a better view, and sure enough it was the backside of a horse. He walked Bess slowly toward the animal talking softly to it as he approached. The saddle and gear appeared to be intact. The horse seemed calm so William was able to ride up to it and take hold of its reins without any difficulty. He scanned the immediate area for any sign of the rider or his footprints, but there was nothing. He then looked the animal over for injuries, but there were only small scratches and scrapes from it's running wildly through the brush. William took some rope and tied the horse to his then led the animal back the way they had come. He crossed the trail he had been on and continued to retrace the tracks of the young chestnut mare that he now led.

About a quarter of a mile further he saw a body lying sprawled on the cold ground. Fearing the worst, he dismounted and slowly approached the body, gently rolling the man over and checking his pulse.

"So you're still alive," William said aloud.

The man was unconscious and it looked like his leg was broke by the way it was bent back. A quick examination of the area seemed to indicate that a coyote had crossed the rider's path, and by the looks of the young horse his guess was that it was freshly broke and probably spooked easily.

Noticing a slight trail that the rider had been on, William figured the best course of action was to follow that trail in hopes of finding shelter since there were no towns or homesteads for several hours the way he had come. The injured man was not heavily dressed and his gear didn't indicate that he would be traveling a long distance so, if he guessed right, the man's home should be relatively close by. He lifted the man and laid him over the saddle of the chestnut before mounting himself and directing Bess down the unfamiliar trail.

Relief swept over him when he saw smoke lifting above the trees just over the next ridge. He spurred Ol' Bess to pick up the pace and in a matter of moments the small log cabin was in sight. He yelled out to the cabin and a young, thin blond-headed woman stepped out of the door with a shotgun in her hands.

"I've got an injured man here…can I bring him on in?" William yelled out with his hands plainly in sight. Even at that distance he could see the life drain out of the woman's face.

She lowered the shotgun and began running towards them. "Oh Jim!" she screamed having obviously recognized the horse and the man's clothing.

"He's alive, but unconscious," William said in an attempt to calm the woman's fears. "We need to get him inside out of the cold," he continued as he dismounted.

"What happened?" she pleaded as she began rubbing the man's face.

"Best I can figure, the horse got spooked by a coyote and bucked him off," William explained as he pulled Jim off of the chestnut and put him over his shoulder. The young woman led them into the small cabin and directed William towards the bed.

William introduced himself to the frightened young lady and tried to calm her down. Elizabeth, as she introduced herself, was a young bride and scared to death that she was soon to be a widow.

William figured the best way to settle her down was to keep her busy. William instructed Elizabeth to remove some of Jim's wet clothes and cover him in a warm blanket as he inspected the man's head. Finding a nasty gash behind his left ear, he instructed Elizabeth in cleaning and dressing the wound.

A couple of hours later, Jim came around but he had no memory of the event or even of what he had done that morning. Elizabeth was beside herself, but William had read a little bit in his medical book of head injuries and felt confident that there was no need to be overly alarmed. The next job at hand, however, was to set that broken leg. Although he had only read about it, he believed he had at least the basic idea of how it was to be done. Nevertheless, he felt sick inside at the thought of doing it.

Feeling that it was important that he show confidence in front of Elizabeth, he simply prayed quietly, explained what he intended to do, then proceeded to reset the leg. Jim's screams of pain caused Elizabeth's tears to flow again but William was confident that his maneuver had been successful. He hoped he never had to go through that again, and he was quite sure Jim felt the same way. William went outside and cut two branches long enough to extend from the injured man's groin to his ankle. He then cut some strips out of a piece of cloth and proceeded to fashion a splint for the broken leg.

It was a while before Jim could sit up due to his pounding head, but eventually he was feeling better and began piecing some things together. He had only recently broken the young mare and she seemed to be coming along well. He remembered riding out that morning to work with her a little bit, but still had no memory of the accident. William explained to Jim where he had found him and the coyote tracks he had seen in the snow.

The two talked about horses and the land while Elizabeth prepared a meal consisting of beef and turnips along with some corn dodgers. Jim's stomach was unsettled so he ate little, but William put away his fair share, being quite satisfied with the young woman's cooking. William expressed his concern over the couple's predicament seeing that Jim would be laid up for a while and with winter well underway. Although the couple initially protested, William convinced them he would gladly stay on for a few days to make sure they had meat and plenty of wood. Inwardly, however, William was struggling. He thought of Laura and his plans to go to her home on the Castor River. Yet, in his heart he knew that the right thing to do was to stay and serve. Do not the Scriptures tell us that Christ came not to be served but to serve? How could William do anything less than his Lord? He must not allow selfishness to rule the day, but trust that the Lord's timing is perfect. His heavenly Father was fully aware of Laura's situation and was able to look after her.

Up early for his daily prayer and meditation, William quietly slipped outside so as not to disturb his hosts. Wrapping his blanket around him, he walked and prayed until the sun began to peak through the trees in the east. He walked over to the woodpile and pulled the axe out of the log where it had been sunk deep to keep the blade clean. Jim had several logs down so William needed only to begin chopping them into pieces suitable for burning in the fireplace. He cut and split for more than an hour before Elizabeth called him in for breakfast.

After some bacon and corn bread, Jim and Elizabeth allowed William to share with them from the Bible. Although they were good and kind people, they knew next to nothing about the Bible or the gospel. William began with John 3:16 and went on to share the story of Jesus' death and resurrection as simply and clearly as he could. William tried to think back to when he had first heard the good news of the gospel, but he was so young at that time that he couldn't really remember not knowing the truth. Nonetheless, he tried to put himself in Jim and Elizabeth's shoes and sympathized with their doubts while patiently answering their questions.

They talked about spiritual things for about thirty minutes before William resumed his wood splitting. Although William was accustomed to work, he rarely worked as long and as hard as he did this particular morning. His heart was invigorated; he felt like the Good Samaritan in Christ's parable recorded in the Gospel of Luke chapter ten, and yet his hands had blistered and formed sores by lunchtime. Somewhat ashamed of his hands, he seemed overly conscious of them as he dipped food and ate.

After lunch, Jim had Elizabeth retrieve his rifle and hand it to William. Along with powder and shot, William took the rifle then saddled Bess to ride. Jim told him of a valley a couple miles west where there was always plenty of deer sign and where Jim had harvested a couple deer in the past. As William rode along, he saw fresh deer sign but knew it was best to hunt further from the cabin so that, in the future, Jim would have game closer to home in case of emergencies.

William had no problem locating the spot Jim had spoken of, and just as the man had said, there was a great deal of sign. William found a good spot to tether Bess well out of site of the place he chose to hunt, then settled in next to an oak tree and waited. It was plenty cool out but there was only a slight breeze. He had taken the breeze into consideration nonetheless and positioned himself downwind to prevent the deer from catching his scent.

William never grew tired of admiring the beauty of God's creation. As the sun was beginning to touch the western horizon, the reddish orange glow gleamed off of the creek running through the valley. He smiled as he watched a couple squirrels chase each other across the forest floor, finally ending up in a tall oak about twenty yards from him, oblivious to his presence. Quietly at first, yet unmistakably, William detected the distinct walk of a deer as the familiar crunch of the leaves grew louder on his left. He sat very still, for although deer can't see nearly as good as a man, they can pick up movement very well, and their hearing is superb.

Finally, he saw the deer out of his peripheral vision and it was heading his way. It was a good sized buck about one hundred and fifty yards away. It was in no hurry and was being very cautious; every few steps it would stop and sniff the air. William waited until the buck was behind some brush and slowly raised the rifle to his shoulder. After a minute or two, the buck stepped out from behind the brush and was almost directly in front of him some seventy-five to eighty yards away. William took a breath and held it for an instant before slowly letting it out as he squeezed the trigger. The rifle bucked in his hands and a puff of black smoke curled from the end of the barrel. The buck jumped and took off running the direction he had been traveling but turning out a bit. William waited quietly for several minutes, then slowly stood and reloaded the rifle. He then made his way to the spot where he had shot. Sure enough, there on the dried leaves were several drops of blood. He had seen the basic direction the deer had gone but stayed with the blood trail noting the regularity of the flow. It looked like he had scored a good hit and it wasn't long before he spotted the downed deer about one hundred yards from where it had been hit. He field dressed it before walking to get Bess.

It was dark by the time he made it back to the cabin so he simply hung the deer from a tree limb and washed up for supper. It was cool enough for the deer to keep overnight; in the morning he would have plenty of light for butchering the animal. Elizabeth had saved him some supper and by the time he had finished he could barely keep his eyes open. It had been a hard day but a good day, and he knew he would sleep well. Before he drifted off to sleep, he whispered a prayer for Laura and entrusted her once again to the care of their heavenly Father.

The whitetail deer provided more than just meat for the frontier family. The sinews or tendons could be removed and dried in order to make strings used for sewing and other various purposes. William had butchered deer in the past but Elizabeth proved to be quite skilled in converting nearly every ounce of the animal into usable material. She even removed the deer's brain and dried it before a fire. She explained that when it had dried she would wrap it tightly in a cloth and wash it vigorously in warm water to make a sudsy solution. She would then wash the raw deer skin thoroughly in the brain water and then pull it over a board until dry. She explained that this process was done a second time using a stronger solution of brain water. Eventually, the skin would be smoked for several hours over a fire of rotten hickory wood. The skin would then be ready to cut into pieces for a shirt or trousers and sewn together with deer sinews. She said that her grandmother had taught her and her sister this process when she was small and she had been given the opportunity to practice many times. William was impressed with the speed and efficiency at which she worked.

William stayed on for a total of four days, having killed another deer and chopped up several rank of wood. Jim and Elizabeth expressed their thanks to William by presenting him with a bone-handled knife that Jim's pa had made. William turned the knife over and over in his hands, admiring the workmanship. William had only been able to acquire four Bibles in Cape Girardeau before starting on his route this go 'round, but he was sure glad that he had gotten some. Jim and Elizabeth accepted a Bible with much appreciation and promised William they would read it. As he left, he assured them that he would check on them in a month or so and would bring some supplies.

Although William was grateful for the opportunity to minister to this family in need, he was ever so glad to be on the trail again. Each step of the horse would bring him that much closer to Laura—and possibly into trouble since he was resolved to face Harrison again.

CHAPTER 25
MIRACLE

Smith Homestead on Castor River, December 1812

Vera had mixed emotions as she turned the letter over in her hands. "This is a letter for Laura from Reverend Travers," Mrs. Bernbaum had said quietly while slipping the letter to her along with some items she was buying from the mercantile. She was sorely tempted to open the letter and read its contents during the ride home, but resolved to respect Laura's privacy. In one sense, she was overjoyed with the letter for it could very well hold the key to releasing Laura from the emotional prison she had found herself in these last several weeks. On the other hand, it might ultimately provide that last nudge to push her family over the precipice that it had been teetering on these last several months. Fear and hope battled each other with each step of her journey home. "Oh God," she prayed quietly, "Please save our family."

Upon entering the cabin she found Laura curled up in her bed as had become routine. It broke her heart seeing her beautiful daughter withering away this way; it seemed that she had lost all desire to live. She looked down at the letter in her hand sensing the firestorm it might potentially release. In that moment, however, she came to a decision and was resolved to face whatever repercussions may come. Vera walked over to Laura and held out the letter.

"I have a letter for you—it's from Reverend Travers," she said while fighting back tears.

Laura sat up quickly and took the letter but held it for a moment as she looked into her mother's eyes. She too sensed the magnitude of this letter. As excited as she was to receive it, there was a flash of fear that nearly caused her to rush over to the fireplace and throw the letter in. What would her father do when he saw the letter? Was her father capable of the things she had only dreamed about? She couldn't bear the thought of anything happening to William.

Vera seemed to understand her daughter's struggle and stated flatly, "Open the letter honey." Laura slowly opened the letter and began to read the contents. Vera watched her daughter's eyes as she read and seemed to actually witness the crumbling of the stronghold that had bound her for so long. The tears began to flow, followed by laughter—it had been so long since she had heard Laura laugh.

Laura handed Vera the letter then stood, putting her hand to her mouth. Vera read the letter and emotion flooded over her as well. She embraced Laura and the two laughed and cried for several minutes before finally stepping back and reading the letter again.

"I'm going to go to him, Ma," Laura stated with an air of determination and resolve that Vera had never seen from her daughter. Although Vera recognized the consequences, she knew in her heart somehow that it needed to be so.

"You do what you feel in your heart is right," she said softly as she placed her hand on Laura's cheek.

Laura quickly packed some personal items and grabbed her coat as she opened the door of the cabin. There before her stood Harrison.

"Where do you think you're going?" he growled, seeing the bag she had packed as he stepped in the door, forcing Laura to step back.

Laura, for the first time in a long time, stepped up to her father and looked him in the eyes. "I'm leaving, Pa…I'm going to see William," she proclaimed boldly.

Harrison's eyes grew ugly and in a flash of rage he reared back and struck Laura square on the chin. Vera's scream filled the cabin and terror gripped her as she watched Laura crumble to the ground in a heap.

Harrison stood looking down at the seemingly lifeless body of his daughter. In that moment, however, Harrison didn't see the limp body of his daughter but another body that lay sprawled on the ground in the same position. He saw the body of his son, Jed! He stared down in disbelief. With his mind's eye he saw the image of his son from nine years ago.

He saw the arrows sticking out from the back of his only son. All over again, he experienced that tremendous sense of loss and deep sadness. In that instant he saw what he had become. What bitterness and hatred he had towards the savages that had killed his son. Yet, with stark clarity, he realized that he himself had become a savage, no different from the very ones that had taken the life of his boy!

Harrison fell on his knees over Laura and began sobbing uncontrollably. The years of pent-up emotions began to flood out of him all at once.

Vera ran to Laura and turned her over. Placing her daughter's head in her lap she sobbed while rocking gently back and forth. Harrison moved to the other side of Laura and began stroking her face. "I'm sorry, Laura… I'm so very sorry," he repeated over and over.

Finally, Laura began to rouse but her eyes widened with fear at seeing her pa over her, suddenly remembering what had just taken place.

"Laura, Laura, it's okay…I'm not going to hurt you," he pleaded. "I'll never hurt you again," he said as he began to sob loudly.

At first Laura lay stunned and speechless. This display of emotion was totally out of character for her father. Then, at the sight of her father's brokenness, it was as if something melted inside of her. An overwhelming feeling of love rose up within her and she wrapped her arms around Harrison and began sobbing herself.

Harrison reached over and took Vera's hand. "I'm sorry, Vera," he whispered. "I've not been the husband or the father that I need to be. Please help me…I want to be the man I should be," he said brokenly. "All I know is hate…please help me learn to love," he pleaded.

Vera embraced Harrison and Laura as she replied, "God can help you Harrison; He is already doing it," she sighed.

CHAPTER 26
TRUE VINE

William En Route to St. Michael, December 1812

William was within an hour of arriving at St. Michael and was feeling a little anxious. "Sometimes it helps to sing," he said aloud. "I shall sing for you, Bess. How does that sound girl?" he said cheerfully.

> *"All glory to God in the sky,*
> *And peace upon earth be restored!*
> *O Jesus, exalted on high,*
> *Appear our omnipotent Lord:*
> *Who meanly in Bethlehem born,*
> *Didst stoop to redeem a lost race*
> *Once more to thy creature return*
> *And reign in thy kingdom of grace"*[10]

"That Charles Wesley sure knew how to write a hymn. Wouldn't you agree, Bess?" William said playfully. "Proverbs 17:22, a merry heart doeth good like a medicine but a broken spirit drieth the bones. I declare, I do feel better, Bess! Bess, if you ever tell folks about our private discussions I'm afraid I may be a little sore with you," William said with a big laugh.

William drew up in front of the mercantile, as was his normal routine upon arriving in St. Michael, and as usual Mr. Bernbaum welcomed him warmly. Soon a messenger was sent out to call all who were able and willing to join Reverend Travers for a service. In the meantime, William eagerly waited for the remaining customers to leave the store so that Mr.

10. Charles Wesley and Lewis Edson, "All Glory to God in the Sky," 1745, Public Domain.

Bernbaum could give him the latest news about Laura. William perused the books on the shelf as he waited.

"That one in particular is a favorite of a certain young lady," Mrs. Bernbaum said suddenly, causing William to jump.

"Oh, Mrs. Bernbaum, you startled me," William said with a blush. "I'm afraid I was miles away in my mind. What was that you said now?" he asked.

"That book that you hold in your hand there," she continued. "That is Laura's favorite. The few times that she was able to come to the store she seemed to always end up standing right there reading that book," Mrs. Bernbaum said with a hint of sorrow. "Believe it or not, it was just this morning that I was finally able to get your letter to Laura's mom," Mrs. Bernbaum whispered. "I ventured out that way a couple of weeks back but Harrison was working around the house and I was afraid to attempt the delivery," she continued. "This morning was the first I had seen of Vera. She was here very early and picked up some supplies, so I slipped her the letter," she concluded.

William considered this and said finally, "My plan is to ride out there after the service."

Mr. Bernbaum had walked up at that moment. "Would you like for me to ride out there with you?" he asked.

"I really appreciate the gesture but I think it's best for me to go alone," William replied. "I honestly feel and believe that God is going to do something amazing," he continued. "I do, however, covet your prayers as I go."

"Of course William," they both said in unison. They looked at each other and laughed. "You see William, when you are married as long as we are then you just think alike!" Mr. Bernbaum roared.

William laughed along with them. This couple tickled his heart. "By the way," William said as he held up the book in his hand, "How much for this book?"

Several people had gathered for the service, but William was nonetheless somewhat disappointed. He had noticed that the numbers were down not only here but pretty much at every stop along his route. It seemed that the effects of the earthquake had diminished in more ways than one. *People are funny,* he thought to himself. *How is it that people can run to God when they are seemingly without hope, frightened or have their life disrupted, but when things are going well it's as if they have no time for Him?* The thought disturbed him. *God doesn't need opportunists,* he thought. *He desires faithful servants who will abide in Him.* William sensed the nudging of the Holy Spirit and although it was only minutes before he was to bring the message he flipped in his Bible to John chapter fifteen and prayed quietly.

"Dear brothers and sisters in the Lord," William began while extending his hands. "I thank you for joining us for the study of God's Word today. In a moment, we shall look at John chapter fifteen together but first let us sing a hymn," William continued. "Sister LaChance, would you care to lead us in 'Rock of Ages'?"

After a few verses of the old hymn by Augustus Toplady, William stood and opened his Bible. John 15:5-6 says, "I am the vine, ye are the branches: He that abideth in me, and I in him, the same bringeth forth much fruit: for without me ye can do nothing. If a man abide not in me, he is cast forth as a branch, and is withered; and men gather them, and cast them into the fire, and they are burned."

"Imagine with me for a moment," William began as he lay his hand on a support beam of the building, "that this beam is the Vine. If you have accepted the Lord Jesus Christ as your Savior, then His blood has cleansed you from your sin and you become a child of God. As His child, you have this wonderful privilege of abiding in Him or remaining in Him. What a joy it is to have a personal relationship with our Savior! I am a child of God because of His grace and mercy. Thanks be to God, I am today abiding in Him," William said, once again making a show of putting his hand on the beam. "But you know, I'm rather busy with my life right now," he said while slightly removing his hand from the beam. "I don't seem to have time to pray or read my Bible for there is simply too many things that I need to do," he continued as he pulled his hand a little further from the pole. "I don't seem to remember the depths from which God has drawn me for now I am simply determined to go my way alone," he stated boldly, finally removing his hand completely from the beam.

Suddenly, he simply collapsed on the floor. Mrs. Bernbaum screamed and began to run to William but he quickly jumped up and laughed. "No, I am fine…I simply wanted to illustrate to you all the danger of forgetting our relationship with Christ," William continued. "If we fail to abide in Him then we begin to die spiritually, just as a branch begins to die when it is broken off of a tree. It is a relationship with Jesus and not just religion that we are living," he exclaimed. "How are we to develop the fruit of the Spirit…love, joy, peace…if we are not spending time with Jesus in prayer and in study of His Word? It must be more than fear of an earthquake that causes us to run to Jesus only to forget Him once the crisis is past!" William pleaded.

"Our sin has separated us from Him and we are in desperate need of his grace and mercy. Thanks to what Jesus did on the cross, we can receive forgiveness. If we have been given so great a salvation, shall we toss it aside like some animal skin that is no longer needed after winter is gone? Heaven forbid, for without Jesus we are spiritually lost! Are you abiding in Jesus today? Do you serve Him regardless of the circumstances life brings your way? He is worthy of your praise and your devotion. He gave His best for you when He died on that rugged cross. Can we not also give our best to Him and remain in His love?" William made an appeal for those who would like to commit their lives to Christ, then after another hymn he closed in prayer.

About halfway through the service, William had noticed a stocky young man walk up to the back of the gathering and listen in. At the appeal, however, he turned and walked away. William felt a twinge in his spirit for something about that man did not seem right. Was it his appearance? No, it was the way he acted perhaps. William shrugged it off but as he left the meeting house he saw the man staring at him from a distance and he had been joined by another hard-faced man who also stood staring. William tried to ignore them and made his way back to the Bernbaums for something to eat before heading out.

"William, you nearly scared me to death this afternoon!" Mrs. Bernbaum scolded as William entered the home. "But I have to say that your illustration was convicting. I fear that I tend to forget the importance of spending time with Jesus regularly. And boy, can I tell it when I do!"

"So can I!" said Mr. Bernbaum, who had just entered the room.

She turned to her husband and swatted him playfully on the arm.

"Hey William, I forgot to tell you about a man I met the other day," Mr. Bernbaum said. "He says there was this sling-wielding circuit rider who happened by and saved their boy! Any idea who this sharp-shooting circuit rider is?" Mr. Bernbaum said with a grin.

"Ah, you have met Edward Tidwell, I presume," William replied.

"Yes, Mr. Tidwell came in the store a couple of weeks back for supplies and told us the story of how you shot that rabid dog with your sling," Mr. Bernbaum explained.

"It's just like little David with his sling in the Bible!" Mrs. Bernbaum added enthusiastically.

"Several folks around town are taking to the name the Tidwells are calling you, 'Sling Shot Circuit Rider,'" Mr. Bernbaum said with a big laugh and a pat on William's back.

"That's just great," William groaned.

CHAPTER 27
TWO AGAINST ONE

Near Mine La Motte, December 1812

It was well into the afternoon before William could get away from the Bernbaums. After a time of prayer together with his friends, William saddled up, took a deep breath, and pointed Bess toward Laura's home. As he headed north out of town, he noticed one of the men he had seen earlier. Once again the man was staring at him, an unnerving stare that disturbed him. Had he seen these men before? He tried to think back to his previous visits to this area but had no recollection of meeting either man. Of course, he had encountered plenty of folks that simply didn't like ministers. On several occasions, he had witnessed people walk up to the crowd gathered only to leave in a huff once they determined that the assembly was for "a religious service." His mind started reenacting some of the more humorous accounts over the last couple of years.

One particular service in New Madrid he would never forget. A couple of teenage boys had wandered by during a service and had stepped in the door to see what was going on. William had been preaching at the time and saw the boys scoff at the message and then leave with several choice words, attempting to be as disruptive as possible. Unfortunately, they did not leave it at that. About a half an hour later they snuck back to a window of the gathering house and threw in a young calf. Chaos ensued to say the least! Of course it was not too humorous then but he couldn't help but laugh thinking about it now. One of the ladies, a Mrs. Gray, screamed and carried on horribly in her efforts to escape the excited calf.

William was so caught up in his reminiscing that he didn't recognize the sound of approaching horses until they were nearly upon him. William turned in the saddle and his heart sank. Riding hard toward him were the two men he had just seen earlier that afternoon in St. Michael. There was no sense in running so he simply turned Bess around and faced them as they reined their horses in front of him.

"Well, well, well…if it isn't the Sling Shot Circuit Rider!" the hard-faced man said sarcastically.

The stocky fellow laughed hoarsely then piped in, "Where you headin', preacher man?"

"Well gentlemen, I'm heading to see a young lady as a matter of fact," William responded coolly.

"That's just what we figured," the hard-faced man responded cruelly. "We have a message for you, little man," he continued as he moved his horse up within an arm's reach of William. "You stay away from Laura!" he yelled, his eyes ugly.

"And what business is it of yours who I visit?" William replied defiantly.

The stocky man stepped his horse up on the other side of William and grabbed hold of Bess's reins. "Let's just say that her pa wants no sissy preacher boy coming 'round and corrupting his daughter," he growled. "And seeing that he is a friend of ours, then that makes it our business," he said, leaning over within inches of William's face.

"What we want to know is if you are smart enough to heed a warning?" the hard-faced man said with a cruel smile.

"Many good men fought and died so that people of this land might be free," William replied. "As an American citizen, I have the right to go where I please," William stated calmly but with determination.

"Well then Mr. fancy talker," the hard-faced man said with a big grin forming on his face, "let's see if you can prove what kind of man you are."

William looked at him for a moment. "Will you allow me to remove my coat?" he asked as he dismounted.

"Why sure, we wouldn't want you to spoil it by getting blood on it," the stocky man replied.

Each man removed his coat and laid it across his saddle then ground hitched their horse. The hard-faced man walked up to face William as the stocky fellow began to circle around behind him.

"It is to be two against one then?" William asked.

"There's nothin' says the fight has to be fair," the hard-faced man said as his right hand came up from his side with such speed that William's move was not quick enough to miss the blow completely. William turned his body with the blow for he knew the stocky man behind him would be attempting to grab him. Sure enough, the man's hands grabbed at his shirt, but William's quick shift to his right prevented the man from getting a good hold. The hard-faced man was quick for he had turned and was launching a left before William was able to get set. The left caught William on his right ear, but, ignoring the blow, he took advantage of the man's open stance and came up hard with an uppercut to the jaw.

Momentarily stunned, the hard-faced man fell back. In that moment, the stocky man rushed into William, knocking him to the ground. Although William rarely boxed, he had wrestled plenty; and where the stocky man thought he had the advantage, William quickly showed him otherwise. William brought his knees up, breaking the man's hold. He then kicked up with both legs, throwing his opponent over his head. The hard-faced man had recuperated and was coming in with both fists ready. William swept his legs in one quick movement, sweeping the man right off his feet. William then came down hard with an elbow into the man's face, and from the sound of the crack, William was sure he'd broken the man's nose. The stocky fellow was coming in again but more warily this time. William jumped to his feet and the two circled momentarily.

Suddenly the man rushed but William side-stepped and tripped the man with his leg. The stocky man went sprawling onto the cold ground, but quickly got to his feet. William wasted no time and grabbed the man before he had a chance to set himself. Doing a quick hip toss, William sent the man squarely into a nearby tree. This time the stocky man was slower in getting up. The hard-faced man's eyes were watering and blood was dripping from his nose, but he was still game. William circled so that the hard-faced man was in between he and the stocky fellow. William feigned a left jab but then immediately shifted to his right, grabbing the man's arm. With one swift movement he swung the man off of the ground and hurled him through the air.

William backed up and waited. The stocky man just stood staring as the hard-faced man got to his feet. For a moment the two just looked at each other. They had obviously misjudged their opponent and were now considering their next move.

The hard-faced man finally frowned and said simply, "I've had enough."

The stocky man was taken back. "Come on Joe, we can take him!" he screamed.

"I've got a broken nose already and I'm just played out," Joe replied miserably as he walked to his horse.

The stocky man just stood there as he debated whether he should have another go at his opponent or simply ride out with his partner. Joe had mounted his horse and sat in the saddle nursing his broken nose.

"You comin' or are you stayin' to get whooped some more," Joe asked sarcastically. After a full minute the stocky man seemed to come to a decision and slowly walked to his horse with his head hanging.

"I never would have believed that I'd be whipped by a preacher man," the hard-faced man exclaimed. He turned his horse and headed out towards St. Michael without ever looking back. The stocky fellow put on his jacket then mounted his horse. He stared at William for several seconds without saying a word, then followed his partner down the trail.

William said nothing but simply stood and watched them until they were out of sight.

William walked over to Ol' Bess and laid his head against the saddle. Now that the fight was over, his body began to tremble as the tenseness began to drain out of him.

"Thank you God for being with me," he prayed quietly. Even though he hadn't really noticed it until now, his ear was ringing where he had been hit. He put his jacket back on then mounted up. Noticing that the sun was beginning to touch the trees in the west, he estimated the amount of time left to reach Laura's home. Mine La Motte was relatively close, so he estimated about an hour of riding if he picked up the pace. It was probably not the best idea to arrive so late in the day, but he simply couldn't stand the thought of waiting another day to see Laura; not to mention the fact that his mentality was such at the moment that he felt ready to face anything, even Laura's father if necessary. Although much of the tenseness had left him, he was still worked up because of the fight.

CHAPTER 28
UNEXPECTED RECEPTION

Laura's Home on Castor River, December 1812

It was nearing sunset when he rode up over the ridge that overlooked Laura's cabin. He felt like a cad arriving at this hour, but was determined to see this through, regardless. Who knows what may have happened today as a result of Laura receiving his letter. He braced himself for the worst then started Bess down the ridge.

"Hello the house," he yelled when he got within fifty feet or so of the cabin.

Harrison opened the door and stepped out holding a rifle. "Who is it?" he called.

"It's William Travers, sir, and I've come to see Laura," William replied boldly.

Harrison stepped off of the porch and headed towards him without saying a word. William's heart began to pound in his chest but he sat perfectly still and waited. To his surprise, Harrison walked up next to William and extended his hand.

"Reverend Travers, welcome," he said simply.

William reached out and took his hand, although halfway expecting Harrison to yank him off of his horse. Harrison stepped back and gestured for William to dismount. Cautiously, and with one eye glued to Harrison, William complied.

"Son, I believe I owe you an apology," Harrison said humbly.

William nearly gasped with shock. His mouth hung open dumbly and he couldn't seem to find his voice.

"I've been a fool...I see that now," Harrison continued. "I have so much anger and bitterness in me that I have let it rule my life since the death of my son," he continued as his gaze drifted to the sunset. "I'm beginning to realize how it's destroying both me and my family. You offered to help me the last time you were here," he said, again turning his eyes to meet William's. "I was wondering if that offer still stands?" he asked sincerely.

William sensed an overwhelming warmth come over him as he realized what this meant. God had truly been at work in this man's heart and, in that instant, it was as if the Holy Spirit removed all resentment and anger he had felt towards Harrison.

"Of course, Mr. Smith, I would be more than happy to," William replied sincerely.

"But first there is a young lady inside who is very anxious to see you," Harrison said with a smile. He motioned for William to follow him and the two walked into the cabin. Laura and her mother stood just inside the door waiting for the men to enter. William removed his hat and greeted the two women cordially. Vera offered William a seat at the table and proceeded to pour him some coffee. Laura, who was all smiles, took a seat next to William.

William suddenly realized that he must look a fright having just left a scuffle as he had. He felt his face flush as he looked down at his stained britches. "I must apologize for my appearance this evening. I fear that I ran into a little trouble on my way here," William said sheepishly.

"What kind of trouble?" Laura asked with sincere concern.

"Well," William hesitated, not quite sure how much to share or how to say it. "I ran into a couple men who...well...we had a disagreement," William finally managed to spit out.

Harrison groaned and lowered his head. "I'm afraid I may be somewhat responsible for your trouble son," he explained with a touch of anguish. "I foolishly spoke with a couple drinking buddies from the mines about..." his voice trailed off as he rose from his chair and walked across the room.

"Reverend Travers, please forgive Harrison," Vera pleaded as she rose from the table to go to her husband. "It has been a rather emotional time for us today," she added meekly.

William felt awkward and confused, not being privy to the obvious dramatic events that had taken place in the Smith home that very day. As curious as he was he was resolved to simply await the details as they may come; he would not ask questions and risk embarrassing his hosts. Laura, too, seemed at a loss for words. She simply stared at her hands as her parents talked quietly in the corner of the small cabin.

Finally, Laura looked up and said in a quiet voice, "I received your letter just this morning. You'll never know what it meant to me," she continued. "Thank you very much for your kind words and encouragement," she concluded as her parents made their way back from their private conversation.

"You could say," Vera added, as she and Harrison seated themselves once more at the table, "that God used your letter to begin a healing in our family. Harrison is a good man, but he has suffered much since the death of our son. We all have suffered a great deal, of course, but my husband has been distant for a while," she looked over at Harrison and laid her hand on his. "But he is home now," she smiled as a solitary tear rolled down her cheek.

Feeling a nudge from the Holy Spirit, William asked his hosts if they would be opposed to him sharing with them from the Word of God. Vera and Laura both sat quietly and waited for Harrison to reply. After a moment or two, Harrison simply nodded so William went outside to retrieve the Bible from his saddlebag. He shared with them the message of God's love and forgiveness and comforted them with the truth that God is able to heal even the deepest hurts. After a time of prayer, William thanked his hosts for their hospitality and excused himself from the table.

Harrison thanked him for his kind words and, due to the lateness of the hour, asked William if he would be opposed to staying the night. "We don't have a lot of room, but we can make up a place in the corner of the cabin; at least it'll be warm and save you a long trip back to St. Michael in the dark," Harrison shared politely.

"I appreciate your kind offer and gladly accept," William replied, grateful for not having to travel at night.

Vera and Laura made a pallet close to the fireplace for William and draped a blanket over a cord to provide him a small amount of privacy.

William felt a little uncomfortable, although he had stayed with many families over the last few years. No doubt it was in part due to Laura being so nearby, but there were also emotions in play here that made him feel he was intruding. Yet, he reassured himself that he had been cordially invited to stay, so he simply removed his boots, reclined on the pallet, and prayed quietly to himself for the Smith family and for the Lord's direction for the coming day. Soon the fatigue of the day's extraordinary events swept over him and he drifted off to sleep.

As was his custom, William awoke at 4:00 a.m. the following morning. He quietly slipped on his boots and donned his coat before silently making his way out the cabin door. He made his way into the barn and checked on Bess before lighting a lantern. Reading from the Psalms he interjected an occasional verse from a hymn before bowing down in an empty stall and calling upon the Lord. As he knelt to pray, William's body reminded him of the fight he was in the day before.

William was so involved in his prayer time that he failed to hear the barn door open nor recognize the entrance of his host. Harrison waited patiently for William to conclude his prayer then shifted slightly to alert William of his presence. William stood and expressed his apologies if he had disturbed the family with his exit so early in the morning. Harrison assured him that no harm was done and that he wished to speak with him privately if he was agreeable. William had once more taken his Bible and explained the way of salvation more clearly to Harrison. Broken and repentant Harrison acknowledged his need of a Savior and William's heart overflowed with joy as he watched Harrison bow his head and accept Jesus Christ as his own personal Lord and Savior. William explained the importance of Bible reading and prayer in order to grow spiritually. The anger and bitterness he had experienced would still attempt to rear its ugly head so he must be diligent about nourishing his new found faith. The two talked for more than an hour before they heard Vera calling them for breakfast. Just before heading into the cabin, William pulled a Bible out of his saddlebag and handed it to Harrison with the instruction to begin reading from the Gospel of John.

There was an air of excitement during breakfast as Harrison shared his decision to follow Christ with his family. Tears flowed freely as Vera and Laura embraced and encouraged him. It was such a tender moment that William felt a hint of embarrassment being witness to it. He halfway rose to slip out in order to give the family more privacy when Vera walked over and hugged him. "We can never thank you enough for all you have done for our family," she shared brokenly. William was touched by the family's willingness to open up to him so freely and had to fight back tears while he finished his breakfast.

After breakfast, William and Laura took a long walk along Castor River. Laura explained in more detail to William the events that had unfolded the day before, interspersed with tearful moments. It was obvious that Laura had been under an enormous emotional strain and it was as if the Lord was in the process of peeling off each painful layer. William sensed the significance of her needing to talk so he simply listened intently and consoled her when the tears came. The two finally made their way back to the cabin and enjoyed a cup of coffee next to the fire; the cool December air had chilled them to the bone.

After a simple lunch William excused himself from the table and again thanked his hosts for their hospitality. He explained that he had a few more stops to make on his circuit and needed to be on his way. Harrison and Vera again thanked William for his ministry to their family then Laura accompanied him outside. Laura walked quietly beside him as he made his way to the barn and saddled Bess. William paused for a moment after he had Bess ready to ride—not sure of what to say. Laura also seemed at a loss for words.

Finally William cleared his throat and looked at Laura. "I meant what I said in the letter concerning my feelings toward you," William struggled. "I know we barely know each other but I hope you will allow me to call upon you as often as I can," William shared sincerely.

"Yes, William," she replied with a smile, "I would like that very much."

"Oh, I almost forgot," William said with a start. "I have something for you," he said as he began digging in his saddlebags. He pulled out a book and handed it to Laura. "I was told that it's a favorite of yours."

Laura took the book with both hands and just stared at it for a long moment before lifting her eyes to meet William's. "Yes, I read this book every time I visit the Bernbaum's store," she said. "I absolutely love this story!" she exclaimed. "Thank you ever so much for thinking of me…it was very sweet of you," she finished as she gently laid her hand on his.

William felt awkward, not knowing how to act or what to say. His stomach had a queer feeling and his mouth became dry. Finally, he managed to find his words, "I read a few pages of the book and…" William swallowed hard then began again, "I read about the prince from the foreign land and the young lady that he pursued."

William took Laura's hand in his and began again with a slight quiver in his voice, "I may not be a prince and neither can I take you on adventures to foreign lands, but I feel in my heart that you are my princess."

A tear formed in Laura's eye and her hand trembled slightly as William continued. "I know we really don't know each other very well yet, and I'll only be able to visit about once a month, but I would like to make my intentions known," he continued. "I hope someday to make you my bride…if you are agreeable," he stated sincerely.

The tear that had welled up in Laura's eye made its way down her cheek and was quickly followed by another. "I don't need a prince from a foreign land," she replied sweetly. "Since the first time I met you at the camp meeting at St. Michael, I knew you were the one God had for me," she continued, wiping the tears from her eyes. "Until you are ready, I'll be waiting," she concluded as she squeezed his hand.

CHAPTER 29
A RENEWED VISION

Cape Girardeau Area, January 1813

William spent Christmas with his family at their farm on the Whitewater River before beginning his route again. His ma was especially thrilled with the news about Laura and encouraged William to plan a wedding in the spring. Although he felt confident that Laura was meant to be his wife, he still wrestled with how to handle marriage and ministry. Should he give up circuit riding and locate somewhere? Many good circuit riders had done so whether due to health reasons or for family. Yet, in his heart, he hated the thought of no longer riding circuit. But would Laura be happy with him gone four to five weeks at a time? He prayed fervently that the Lord would order his steps in this matter.

The first week of the New Year found William in the saddle again and making his way along his route. It was quite cold and the winter wind seemed to blow right through him. There would be little sleeping outdoors in this weather; at least he hoped that folks would be kind enough to put him up for the night. He had picked up some extra supplies for Jim and Elizabeth before he left Cape Girardeau, since he knew they would be in desperate need of them soon with Jim laid up with that broken leg the way he was. As he rode, he reminisced about the events over the last year.

Both from the visit with his family and the news he heard in town, it sounded like the war efforts were not going as favorably as many had hoped. Much of the recent fighting was taking place to the north and east of them near a place called Detroit, with little taking place anywhere near Missouri, save some random Indian attacks. There were those, even still, who were concerned about the results of the war and its impact on the young country. An interesting bit of information being discussed was that Tecumseh had been commissioned a brigadier general in the British army and was active in the fighting near Detroit. The war did, in fact, affect the Missouri Territory in more indirect ways than fighting—or lack thereof. The fear of renewed Indian raids, along with the general threat of war, seemed to be impeding territorial development and expansion. Fewer families moving into the area was not the only change being felt, however. Commerce was being negatively impacted both from local merchants joining the militia and difficulty in securing or shipping supplies. Basically, it was getting more difficult to get supplies, and as a result, prices were going up. Furthermore, there were concerns that the fur trade, which was an important business in the Missouri Territory, was being impacted due to increased tensions with the Indians. All in all, there was a twinge of fear and concern among those with whom William had spoken during his visit home.

The year of 1812 had not only been eventful due to the war, but the reoccurring shocks from the earthquake had left an indelible imprint on the region and even the nation. It was being reported that shaking had been felt as far north as the Great Lakes and clear to the Atlantic seaboard on the east! Someone in Cape Girardeau had said that he felt the shock clear in Washington D.C. while he was there on business. The impact, however, had been especially traumatic on those in and around the New Madrid area. Settlements such as Little Prairie, where William had been when the first shock hit, were now virtually abandoned. The emotional impact had been significant as well, with remnants of it still felt even now.

Another noteworthy historical event of 1812 pertained to a more political element concerning the region. William had heard talk months before but obtained more details during his recent visit. On the 4th day of June, just fourteen days before war was declared on the British, Missouri was officially organized into a territory with a governor and general assembly. From here on out the region would be officially known as the Missouri Territory. Prior to this, the region was known as the Upper Louisiana section of the Louisiana Territory, although some would refer to it as Missouri due its proximity to the Missouri River. The name change was mostly due to Louisiana becoming a state, hence the need to rename the remaining sections of the territory. But more than the name change, the reorganizing of the territory from the first or lowest class to a second class territory with a governor and legislature meant self government and progress. It was a notable step in the advancement of the territory in which William called home.

William found Jim and Elizabeth in good health, but in much need of the supplies that he had brought. Jim was able to walk around some with a crutch he had made but was not quite ready for the daily routine of frontier life. To help out, William busied himself cutting more firewood while Elizabeth prepared a meal using provisions he had supplied. William was pleased to learn that the couple had been reading the Bible he had left with them. They were also full of questions so William talked with them well into the evening hours. His hosts were gracious enough to invite him to stay the night, which he did happily. He appreciated his new friends and felt at home with them. This was not at all the case with several of the families along his route. After a warm breakfast and hot coffee the next morning, he wished them well and continued on his route.

The next two weeks held some unique challenges for William. First, there was the weather which was unusually brutal. The bitter winds were an everyday struggle for both he and Ol' Bess. She was no longer a young mare and he feared that this might be the last year he would enjoy the circuit with his old friend. His fears were realized when one morning he awoke to find Bess lying lifeless on the cold ground. Compounding his sorrow was the reality that he was halfway through his circuit route and now without transportation. The family with whom he had stayed the night before had no horses to spare, but agreed to take him to the next settlement so he might find one. Before they left, William stood over Bess for a moment and thanked God for the time he had been given with his old riding companion. "She was a faithful friend," he said simply as they loaded in the wagon and headed out.

On top of his horse troubles, he also experienced lodging inconveniences. His search for an available horse led him off his normal route as well as his schedule. Once he was able to procure another steed, he found himself in an area somewhat unfamiliar to him. He pushed on as long as he could, but the lateness of the hour, along with the freezing temperatures necessitated immediate shelter. Unfamiliar as he was with his present location, he plodded on while fervently praying that he would run into a cabin soon. The sun had already set by the time he caught the scent of wood smoke. He picked up the pace and finally found a tiny cabin nestled in a grove of willows.

The homesteader owned a dog, which warned its owner of the approaching stranger so he was immediately met by a warning hail.

"Who goes there and what's your business?" came the gruff call from the inside of the cabin.

William's lips were so cold that he feared he would be unable to reply. Thankfully, he was able to make himself heard and was approached by a large bearded man wrapped in a buffalo hide and holding a gun.

"I'll see no man freeze to death in this weather," he said flatly. "You can put your mount in the barn there and after you've seen to him then come on in the house," he said shortly, then turned and walked back to the cabin.

William wiped the young, spirited gelding down and found a feed bag, putting it on him before heading to the house. The man pointed to some grub on a small table in the middle of the room but never looked up or spoke. William downed the tasteless grub and was thankful for it in spite of the little that it was. He attempted to spark a conversation a couple different times but it was obvious that his host had no desire to oblige.

Finally, William rolled out his bedroll on a bare space near the fireplace and tried to relax. Since entering the cabin, he had detected an unusual odor but only now did it seem to register. The odor radiated from the man himself. When the man passed him to go to bed William nearly heaved. He couldn't help but wonder when the man had last taken a bath, if he ever had! If that wasn't enough he then felt something crawling on his arm and then his head. From the firelight he inspected his arm and with amazement realized that it was bedbugs! He was never more happy to see daybreak as he was that next morning. He may have dozed off and on for a short time but he was quite sure that he had slept less than an hour throughout the night. As soon as it was light enough to ride, he rolled up his bedroll, thanked his host for the accommodations, and wandered out into the cold. He quickly saddled the young gelding and hurried on down the trail with nary a look back.

His new horse was a beauty, a chestnut gelding with a blaze on its nose. It was also very spirited, which would take some getting used to since Ol' Bess had been quite calm. He had little money with him but was blessed that the family where he had stayed fronted him some funds so he could make the purchase. It had pained him to even ask, but the family was very kind and more than willing to help. "You've done so much for us the last year or so that it is about time we have the opportunity to repay you in some small way," the man had said sincerely. By the time William had reached St. Michael, he was finally beginning to get a feel for the new mount.

He was pleased to find that a primer he had left with the church was being put to good use. One of the ladies in the congregation had decided to begin teaching the children of the settlement just that week. There were only four students but it was a start. He had noted along the circuit this time around that three or four families where he had left a primer were beginning to utilize the resource at home. The desire for education was encouraging for it would only serve to help build the local communities and the region as these young people gained wisdom and knowledge; not to mention the advancement of the gospel as each individual could read the Bible on their own!

Over lunch with Mr. and Mrs. Bernbaum, William recounted the events surrounding his trip to the Smith homestead the month prior. The reaction from Mrs. Bernbaum was especially entertaining for William. She squealed and clapped her hands with excitement one minute then began to cry the next. Mr. Bernbaum was curious about the two miners who had jumped William during his ride to see Laura. The one named Joe, who had ended up with a broken nose, had given him a bit of trouble some time back in the mercantile. He fully intended to spread the word on the two in case they were planning anything else.

"The citizens of St. Michael will not indulge such behavior I assure you," Mr. Bernbaum exclaimed passionately.

William went on to share with his friends his conversation with Laura.

Mrs. Bernbaum was giddy with excitement, "I had a feeling about you two from the start."

He also explained his reservations in marrying right away, only to abandon his wife at home the bigger part of the year. The Bernbaums were very sympathetic to his concerns and offered to pray with him before he continued on his way. They also promised to pray for William each morning during their devotion time. *Friends are a rare treasure in life,* he mused as he pointed the gelding north toward the Smith homestead on the Castor River.

Laura was walking back to the house from the barn when William topped the ridge overlooking the homestead.

"Hello the house," he yelled then trotted the horse down the ridge.

Laura gleamed with delight as she ran to meet him. William's heart seemed to skip a beat when she took his hand and welcomed him. *It is something how a woman affects a man,* he thought to himself. It was a feeling that both frightened him but excited him all at the same time. He realized now what his dad had tried to explain to him several years ago, "once you experience a woman's love, you can never really be content without it."

"What happened to Bess?" Laura asked suddenly as it struck her that William was on a different mount.

"I'm afraid that I lost her a couple weeks back," William said solemnly.

"I'm very sorry for you. I know you two were a good team," she shared sympathetically. "This looks like a fine horse though," she continued as she circled the gelding. "Have you given him a name yet?" she asked curiously, scratching the horse's ears. The young gelding, enjoying the attention, nuzzled her gently.

"Actually, I hadn't really thought about it too much," William confessed. He stood studying for a minute as he looked over the horse. "Now that I think about it, that blaze looks somewhat like a lightning bolt so perhaps 'Lightning' would be a good name; it certainly matches his personality too, as a matter of fact!" William said with a smile.

"I like it…Lightning. That's a fitting name," she added agreeably. The two then made their way to the cabin as Laura chattered away about the events that had taken place since William's last visit.

William was encouraged by the news that Harrison had been attempting to read the Bible most everyday, in spite of his many questions. This, of course, pleased William even more, for how many individuals had he encountered who were quick to say they read their Bible regularly, yet lacked the sincere desire to actually learn from what they were reading and put it into practice. William opened his Bible and spent nearly an hour with the family discussing truths from God's Word, being careful to respond to each of Harrison's questions the best way he knew how. There were some, however, that he confessed he did not know himself but would endeavor to find the answer to before his next visit.

William was once again invited to stay the night, to which he heartily agreed. He looked forward to spending some time alone with Laura the next morning. He and Harrison checked on the animals before retiring for the evening. While at the barn, they entered into another lengthy discussion which solicited a couple of concerned calls from the house before they finally managed to wrap it up. William was sincerely amazed at the noticeable change in the man that could only be attributed to the fingerprint of the Almighty.

After a warm breakfast, Laura and William strolled along the banks of the Castor River as they talked about the weather, farming, horses, and the crops that would be planted that spring. The hours sped by in spite of the cold temperatures. William couldn't get over how easy she was to talk to and it saddened him terribly to think of leaving her again. For a moment he considered again the issue of matrimony and frowned slightly at the mental picture that flashed in his mind of the long hours away from each other and especially of Laura at home alone. His reaction did not go unnoticed, however, and Laura questioned him on it immediately. In that instant he decided that it would be best to share with her his struggles so that they could simply pray about it together. To his surprise, she reacted little to his concerns for, she explained, she had sensed them already. She, too, had considered this and would not in any way want to hinder him in the ministry that God had given him.

"Have you entertained the thought," she proposed, "that perhaps we could build a cabin close to my folks here on the Castor River? That way I could still be close to my family when you are traveling and you needn't worry about me," she said with a slight turn of the head and a wrinkled lip.

It seemed so obvious, yet the thought had never really struck him. William smiled as he replied, "I think that's a wonderful idea!"

Without warning they both began to chuckle and then it turned into outright laughing. The joy they both felt in their heart simply could not be contained. They literally ran back to the cabin so that William could fulfill the gentlemanly custom of asking Harrison's permission for his daughter's hand in marriage. It came as no surprise to either him or his wife and the four celebrated together before it came time for William to leave.

Before he left, they decided that the wedding date should be scheduled for mid-April and that it would be held at St. Michael. William felt confident that his family would be happy to make the trek with him for the festivities. He was so excited for his family to meet Laura and knew that his ma would simply adore his bride to be. Harrison offered to begin work on a cabin as soon as the weather broke, and he was sure that some of the neighbors would gladly chip in and assist him.

The remainder of the circuit found William all smiles and in good spirits. When he wasn't daydreaming about the wedding and he and Laura's new life together, he was reading once again the Journal of David Brainerd which his dad had bought for him from his uncle Zeb several years back now. The book was well worn since he kept it with him most of the time, and he was sure that he had read it through at least a dozen times. The stories and personal accounts from this missionary to the American Indians in the mid 1700s never ceased to encourage and inspire him. As a matter of fact, outreach to the Indians was always something near and dear to his heart.

Intermingled with his daydreaming and his reading, he began to pray for Komoka. He suddenly felt an overwhelming sense of urgency to pray at one point so he tethered his horse to a nearby sapling, knelt down by a tree, and began to intercede for his Indian friend. He must have prayed for a good half hour, for his toes were numb when he finally stood. As William mounted Lightning, he pondered about Komoka's whereabouts and what his friend may be encountering. As he rode the remaining half day's ride into Cape Girardeau, another thought was birthed in his heart. He considered how many families along his present circuit were responding favorably to the Bibles and primers. He wondered at the possibility of incorporating Komoka's assistance in approaching some of the more "white-man friendly" tribes in the area; perhaps they would be open to the same service along with ministering the Word to them. He had ministered only a little to the Delaware tribe just south of Little Prairie, for even among these who were friendly with the white man, they were still somewhat reserved and guarded with him. Perhaps with the assistance of one of their own it could open some doors.

All of a sudden, he was struck with the realization that he wasn't even sure if Komoka was a Christian. It embarrassed him to even think it for he, being a minister, should have at least posed the question to his friend. That was a problem that he would soon remedy if he could convince Elder Parker of the merit of such a venture. The possibility invigorated him as he pondered on it further. Was not the gospel for every tribe and nation? Surely God could open doors for him to minister to the Indian as well as his fellow white man!

CHAPTER 30
SEEKING THE LORD'S DIRECTION

Cape Girardeau, Early February 1813

William couldn't wait to visit with Elder Parker about his idea of outreach to the Indians so he headed straight to Cape Girardeau without first stopping by his folk's house on the Whitewater River, which was his normal routine. He knew he wasn't guaranteed to see his mentor and friend since he traveled a great deal, being elder over the Indiana district, which included Indiana, Illinois, and Missouri territories.

It was with relief that he saw Elder Parker outside gathering firewood. Upon seeing William, the good elder immediately lowered his armload of wood and made his way to greet him as he dismounted. Elder Parker recognized the absence of Ol' Bess right away so William had to tell his sad tale once more. Of course, the elder had to inspect the new horse, which ultimately met his approval. He also thought the name was fitting. The two then made their way out of the cold and into the warm house where they enjoyed a hot cup of tea. William proceeded to share with Elder Parker about his plans to marry which was met with much excitement and congratulations. His mentor was a great comfort to him as he shared about his ongoing concerns about marriage and ministry. The elder's advice and encouragement only served to reinforce William's decision to marry and proceed with the wedding plans.

William then began opening up about his desire to locate Komoka and initiate plans to reach out to the Indians. Elder Parker listened intently, without interrupting, until William had shared all that was in his heart. William sat impatiently as his mentor sat and studied on the matter for what seemed like a very long time.

Finally, Elder Parker stood and walked to a window and looked out before speaking. "I have had a similar desire as you son, for it is true that the Indian is made in God's image, just as we are," he began. "But to be honest with you, I have some concerns about your plan at this particular time," he continued as he turned to face William. "As you are fully aware, we are in the middle of a war in which some Indians are aligned with our enemies. Those Indians who are opposed to this action are nonetheless impacted by it. Many Americans, either out of general fear or ignorance, have reacted strongly to all Indians and tensions are high…on both sides. I'm in favor of your idea, but I'm not sure that now is the right time to execute it; quite honestly, I fear for your safety," he concluded.

He saw the disappointment in William's face but no rebuttal or resistance was forthcoming. William had proven himself to be a faithful servant of the Lord and one that seemed to be sensitive to the leading of the Holy Spirit. Perhaps he was being too hasty.

"William, I'll tell you what we should do," Elder Parker added, as he raised a finger in the air and walked towards him. "I do not want to allow my own judgment to precede God's direction so let's spend some time in prayer about this. Please spend a few days with your family, but make time each day to intercede about this, and I will do the same. Meet me back here in three days time and we will discuss this further," he said with a smile.

William stood to his feet and thanked his mentor for hearing him out and for his guidance. The two prayed together before William made his way out of Cape Girardeau along the trail to his parent's house along the Whitewater River.

Jacob was working on a wagon wheel when William rode up. "Having troubles, Pa?" he asked as he removed his tack and began carrying it towards the barn.

"I'm gonna ban your ma from using the wagon if this keeps up," he said, barely taking time to look up from his work. "This is the second time in six months that woman has taken it to town and brought it back needing repairs," he grunted.

"I'll be glad to help you, Pa, but I have some news that I would like to share with you and Ma first...if you don't mind," William yelled over his shoulder as he walked into the barn.

Jacob laid down his tools and met William at the front of the house. "Gives me a good reason to take a break," he said with a smile as he patted William on the back. "Good to see you, Son," he said as he opened the door for William.

Sarah had been baking, and the smell of fresh baked bread filled William's nostrils as he and his pa stepped into the warm house.

"Boy, does that smell heavenly," William said with a sigh of satisfaction. "A person gets tired of jerked meat on the trail every day for a month!" he exclaimed as he headed straight to the kitchen and reached for the bread.

"Now William, my guess is that Mrs. Bernbaum, and some of those other nice ladies along the trail that you've told me about, gave you more than jerked meat," Sarah quipped as she hugged her son. "How are you son?" she asked as she helped William with the warm bread.

"The boy says he has some news for us, Sarah," Jacob boomed as he seated himself at the table.

Sarah could not contain her excitement as she took a seat and fidgeted impatiently. "This would not concern a certain young lady would it?" she asked with a sneaky grin.

"Now Sarah, let the boy speak his mind," Jacob scolded.

With great delight, Sarah and Jacob listened as William shared his plans to marry Laura in the spring. The tears flowed freely as Sarah expressed her sincere happiness for William. Jacob offered a firm hand shake of congratulations as the two made their way outside to work on the wagon. William was reluctant to mention his desire to first track down Komoka and initiate plans to reach out to the Indians. There was no need to spoil the moment or worry his folks, at least not until he was absolutely sure this was truly God's plan for him. He had felt so sure on the trail that this was the leading of the Holy Spirit but he greatly admired Elder Parker and trusted his wisdom. Yes, he would seek God's face these three days to make sure that this was not simply personal feelings and ambitions getting in the way.

Each morning, William set aside extra time to pray specifically for Komoka and the Indian outreach idea. He would also slip away in the evenings and find a quiet place to seek the face of God. During the day, he worked with his pa around the farm and even helped on a few pair of shoes that Jacob had been working on. *Never hurts to maintain learned skills*, William mused. Although some would consider it tedious, he actually enjoyed the work and found it relaxing to work with his hands. Jacob had been saddened by the news of the death of Ol' Bess. The trusty mare had been with them since their days in Kentucky and had been a faithful friend. The two talked at length about the land around St. Michael and of William's future in-laws. Jacob looked forward to seeing the country and especially meeting Harrison. The stories William had told of the man had piqued Jacob's interest and he was anxious to swap yarns with him.

William also made time to visit his brother, John, and his young bride, who were expecting a child already. Their excitement about becoming parents was clearly evident. John was a farmer, but during the winter months he kept himself busy working out in a shed he and Jacob had built behind his house. William's younger brother had become quite adept at working with wood and was beginning to get occasional requests from folks in the area to make them pieces of furniture. It was commonly thought that the more furniture and belongings a person or family owned, the higher their social status. Land was so plenteous here, west of the Mississippi, that the amount of land owned did not necessarily equate to being "well off." *Little brother has taught himself a trade that should have a good future*, William thought to himself as he made the trek back to his folk's house along the Whitewater River.

The three days at home with his family were rejuvenating for William even though they passed too quickly. It was such a good feeling to have a place of refuge where you feel loved and accepted. The new territory was still very much untamed with crime prevalent and a lack of adequate law enforcement. With the ever present threat of Indian attack and persecution from the more ruthless element of society, it had a way of draining a man's spirit. The time spent with his family in a relaxing environment provided the best atmosphere for which to seek God's guidance concerning his future ministry. On the evening of the second day, William sensed the Lord's presence in such a sweet and intimate way; it reminded him so much of those special moments he spent with the Savior as a boy back in Logan County, Kentucky. Sure, he acknowledged the Lord's guidance and presence with him as he traveled the circuit, but there was something special about simply sitting at the feet of the Savior. He recalled the story in the Scriptures about Mary and Martha, and too often he resembled Martha in her zeal to serve but to the neglect of simply resting in the Lord's presence.

The tears flowed freely as he unloaded his cares and concerns at the feet of his Savior. And yet, it was the morning of the third day that William really felt like he received a confirmation concerning his desire to begin an outreach to the Indians. He was reading in the book of Acts as he began his quiet time and arrived at the passage concerning Philip's encounter with the Ethiopian eunuch in chapter eight. The words almost jumped off the page at him as he read about the divine appointment God arranged between these two men. Philip had basically left an out-and-out revival in Samaria because the Lord directed him to go out into the desert. And yet, Philip obeyed the Lord and on the desert road had a chance encounter with an official from Ethiopia who, of all things, was reading a passage of Scripture. The Spirit of the Lord directed Philip to go up alongside the chariot where he overheard the man reading a passage out of Isaiah. Philip asked the foreigner if he understood what he was reading then proceeded to explain Christ to him from that very passage—leading ultimately to the Ethiopian eunuch being saved! He remembered hearing Reverend McGready mention that history bears witness to the fact that this same Ethiopian man went on to bring the gospel to his homeland and impacted many lives as a result. In that moment, William's heart felt as if it might burst within him as he sensed the Holy Spirit confirming that Komoka and he had a divine appointment to keep.

The morning of the fourth day found William in the saddle and on his way to visit Elder Parker. A glint of doubt brushed his mind that perhaps his mentor would still see things differently. And yet, he felt more sure than ever that this was the leading of the Lord, so resolved to simply trust that the same God who confirmed it to him in such a real way could and would most assuredly do the same in the heart of his friend.

The good elder was not at all surprised to see William arrive early at his door. The tremendous smile across Elder Parker's face immediately sent a flood of relief over his heart although his mentor did not yet say a word. The two sat down for a cup of coffee and the elder led them in a time of prayer and thanksgiving. Only then did his mentor begin to discuss the topic for which they both had prayed so fervently the past three days.

"William," Elder Parker began, "I apologize for being so hasty in my judgment the other day. You would think that a man my age would have learned by now not to rush in front of God," he said with a smile. "I'm fairly confident that I know how the Lord has spoken to you over the last three days" he continued, "so please indulge me for a few moments while I share with you my experience."

Elder Parker stood and walked over to the window looking out. When he began to speak his voice was cracked and broken, "I was in the middle of my morning devotion yesterday when I felt an overwhelming sense of the Holy Spirit's presence," he said quietly. "So few of the Indian peoples have been reached with the gospel," he continued as he turned and walked across the room. "The Bible says that there will be people in heaven someday from every tribe, nation, and tongue; but how will they get there unless they receive the good news of the gospel of Jesus Christ?" he said passionately. "These are things we know and preach and yet the reality of everyday life seems to keep us blinded to the fact that there are many who have not yet heard!" he exclaimed. "Common sense says that now is not the time to approach the Indians," he said more quietly as he once again sat down across from William, "but I believe the Lord has a special appointment for you to keep with this Indian friend of yours."

"In some way," he paused, trying to fight back tears, "I believe that God has something in store for your friend…God is going to use him in some way. This is what I felt the Lord spoke to me during my devotions yesterday morning," Elder Parker concluded.

William was unable to contain his surprise and awe. His mouth hung open dumbly and he couldn't decide whether to stand or sit, to laugh or cry. He felt overwhelmed by it all. He would never cease to be amazed at how the Holy Spirit directed the lives of men—those who would seek His face. Suddenly, William began to laugh for there was such joy that welled up in him. He had no illusions as to the difficulty and danger with the task before him but he would be proceeding down the path God had laid for him. With that knowledge came such peace and fulfillment. What a privilege God gives to these earthen vessels that we can be used by the Master to proclaim the message of His truth and love. Both men laughed and prayed together, then began to make plans for William's journey. Not only were supplies required for his trip, but an alternate circuit rider would be needed for at least a portion of his circuit. He also needed to write Laura, who he hoped would not take the news too hard. He fully expected that their wedding plans for the spring would continue as scheduled but she would, no doubt, be somewhat upset and concerned about his seemingly haphazard plans without her prior knowledge. Elder Parker committed to assigning another circuit rider for his route in the next couple of weeks and assured William that his letter would arrive at St. Michael within the month. Once the logistics of William's trip were in place, the good elder placed his hands on William's shoulders and quoted the first several verses of Psalm 91 from memory:

"He that dwelleth in the secret place of the most High shall abide under the shadow of the Almighty. I will say of the Lord, He is my refuge and my fortress: my God; in him will I trust. Surely he shall deliver thee from the snare of the fowler, and from the noisome pestilence. He shall cover thee with his feathers, and under his wings shalt thou trust: his truth shall be thy shield and buckler. Thou shalt not be afraid for the terror by night; nor for the arrow that flieth by day; Nor for the pestilence that walketh in darkness; nor for the destruction that wasteth at noonday. A thousand shall fall at thy side, and ten thousand at thy right hand; but it shall not come nigh thee. Only with thine eyes shalt thou behold and see the reward of the wicked. Because thou hast made the Lord, which is my refuge, even the most High, thy habitation; There shall no evil befall thee, neither shall any plague come nigh thy dwelling."

"Go with God, my son, and know that I will be covering you with my prayers throughout your journey," Elder Parker said finally as William mounted Lightning and headed back to his folk's house.

His parent's reaction was as William had expected, but after a time of sharing with them of the events leading up to the decision they seemed to soften some. To a certain extent, they had already been forced to commit William completely into God's care, for the circuit rider's life was one of continual risk. But to be a parent, William understood, is to be concerned for a child's safety, even if they are grown. With that in mind, William did his best to answer their concerns and assure them of God's clear direction. Before departing, he knew that his two best prayer partners would be lifting his name continually before God's throne. He finished preparing his supplies and headed south toward New Madrid.

CHAPTER 31
INDIAN VILLAGE

New Madrid Area, February 1813

The ride from Cape Girardeau to New Madrid along King's Highway brought back good memories. Upon arriving at New Madrid, he visited some of the families that he had come to know and love during his days of riding the New Madrid circuit. While riding along to another stop in town, he heard an unfamiliar sound down by the river. His curiosity got the better of him so he steered his horse toward the sound. As soon as the river came into view he caught a glimpse of the source of the strange noise. Approaching the dock was a large boat unlike any boat he had ever seen before. He found a place to tether his horse then joined a small crowd that was making their way towards the incoming craft. Spotting Mr. Gray, a parishioner he knew from the New Madrid Methodist church, he made his way over to join him.

"Well, Reverend Travers, it's been a long time!" Mr. Gray said enthusiastically. "It's wonderful to see you, how have you been?" he continued.

"Very well, sir," William replied, "how about you and Mrs. Gray?"

"We are all doing fine, very fine," he replied joyfully. Noticing William's fascination with the large watercraft, Mr. Gray remarked, "Have you ever seen anything like it?"

"No sir," William responded, "but to be honest with you, I'm not completely sure what I'm looking at."

"That's a steamboat my boy!" Mr. Gray proclaimed excitably. "A man by the name of Fulton invented a boat like this one back in 1807. Named it the *Clermont*. For a while there was some talk about bringing the *Clermont* to the Mississippi River but it has been put to use on the Hudson River back East instead. It was sometime in 1811, I guess, that a company out of Pittsburgh built this here boat. They call it the *New Orleans*. It has been making trips from Pittsburgh clear to New Orleans the last year or so now," he continued as he grabbed William by the elbow and began leading him closer to the boat. "Come on and get a better look," he said enthusiastically.

The large boat was in dock now and some men were disembarking with cheers going up from the crowd of onlookers. "They say," Mr. Gray continued with one armed raised waving at the newcomers, "that this here steamboat has remarkable advantages over the keel-boat. The claim is that they can not only shorten the travel time, but also lower the expense of transportation. If that's true, then we are bound to see more and more of them on the Mississippi with so much being shipped to New Orleans," he exclaimed.

William was somewhat embarrassed having not yet seen the steamboat, although he had read some accounts about them over the last year. "I've been ministering farther north of late so although I've read some about the new marvel, this is the first one I have had the privilege of inspecting," he explained sheepishly. Mr. Gray explained that although the *New Orleans* had made several trips down the Mississippi, it, nor any other steamboat, had yet to venture further north on the Mississippi River than the mouth of the Ohio River. Therefore, it was little surprise that William had yet had the opportunity to see this example of man's ingenuity.

Being somewhat later in the day, William accepted Mr. Gray's invitation to dine with them as well as spend the night. Initially committed to keep his plans private, he was nonetheless pressed to the point that he finally divulged his destination to his curious hosts. At once, he knew it to be a mistake for the two criticized him severely for "such a foolish venture." Although the Gray's were good people and did not mean to hurt him, their negativity was like a heavy weight on William's heart. Sleep came slowly and was restless, once it did come. Nevertheless, he thanked his hosts the next morning and continued his journey.

The directions he had received from Komoka, several months ago now, were general at best. From New Madrid he was to travel a day's ride west by southwest until he reached where the St. Francis River turned east then north for a ways before then returning to its natural southward flow. Just below this southward bend of the river, he was instructed to locate a bluff with white clay that resembled chalk. This bluff was along the ridge that runs southwesterly from well up into the Missouri Territory for several miles in the direction of the Arkansas River. Komoka had told him that their village was just on the other side of the river and only a couple miles west of the bluff he had described. There was a rough trail that William followed for several hours, but he began struggling into the afternoon hours when the trail became more difficult to make out. His fear was that he would veer too far north or south and totally miss any of the landmarks Komoka had described to him. He would then be hard-pressed to find the village before dark and he was not eager to spend the night alone this deep in Indian country. He prayed quietly to himself as he searched in vain for a more prominent trail or for any sign of assurance that he was going in the right direction. William's heart sank lower and lower in his chest as the sun drew ever closer to the horizon.

As he continued westward, his thoughts wandered back to the day that he first met Komoka. He smiled to himself when he pictured Komoka watching him shoot at the squirrel with his sling. Regardless of the language barrier, the two seemed to form an instant connection. What fun they had so long ago using the sling and shooting Komoka's bow. His mind reenacted the events back at his family's campsite and how proud he had been to demonstrate his skill to Komoka's father with his handmade weapon. He remembered well the moment Komoka presented him with the amulet, recognizing only years later the significance of such a gift. He hesitated referring to it as an amulet for, although the Indian may believe it in some way made his hunt successful, it was merely a collection of animal remains attached to a rawhide strap. It was, however, given to a young brave from a wise and loving grandfather which made it special indeed. With a glint of humility, William recognized what made the gift from Komoka such a significant act—it was a sincere gesture of friendship, not from one Indian boy to another Indian, but to a white boy!

Thinking of the special gift prompted William to pull it from his saddle bag and, running it through his fingers, look it over anew. The original rawhide strap had to be replaced but the bear claw, tooth of a mountain lion, and feather from an eagle all were the original components making up the treasured gift.

He was lost in his thoughts when he sensed movement to his left. The horse's ears went up and its body tensed, but before William could react, several Indian braves appeared from the ground like ghosts. At least five warriors surrounded him with bows drawn and all William could do was wait. To run or even move was to die. "Lord help me," he whispered softly as he sat perfectly still in the saddle. The expression on the warrior's face directly in front of him made William's blood curdle. He could almost feel the man's hatred and with a sudden shock of realization, he knew that this warrior meant to kill him. He watched the man's fingers holding his bowstring with arrow ready; an arrow aimed at his heart. Suddenly, a sharp command came from an older warrior to William's right and immediately the warriors lowered their weapons, all except the warrior directly in front of him. Another command was given, more forceful this time, and slowly the warrior in front of him lowered his bow but kept his hard eyes fixed on William.

The Indian who had spoken walked toward William and took the amulet from his hand. Inspecting the ornament briefly he returned his gaze to William and asked forcefully in broken English, "Where you get this?"

Although his heart was racing and his palms sweaty, despite the cold February weather, William spoke clearly and confidently, "I received this amulet as a gift from my Indian friend, Komoka."

At the name Komoka, William detected a reaction from the older Indian, howbeit ever so slight. The Indians spoke excitedly amongst themselves for a few moments until finally one Indian took the reins of William's horse and began leading him ahead. Not a word was spoken as two other braves fell in behind William and the others disappeared into the woods. William knew better than to try to run, so he simply sat quietly and with curiosity considered what lay before him.

Within an hour they reached what he believed was the St. Francis River. One of the Indians forcefully pulled William from the saddle and

directed him towards one of several canoes lined up along the bank. Two
of the braves entered the canoe with him and pushed off from the bank
with the third Indian standing holding the reins to William's horse. A hint
of sadness struck him as the horse diminished from his sight. Would he
ever see Lightning again? Would he ever see Laura and his family again?
He would not allow fear or despair to conquer his heart. *He is my refuge
and my fortress: my God, in him will I trust*; the words from Elder Parker's
recitation of Psalm 91 comforted him and gave him confidence.

Upon crossing the river, the three began walking westward with one
Indian in the lead, the other behind, and William in the middle. They had
not bound his hands, nor were they cruel with him yet not a word was
spoken. They continued their silent march for close to an hour before
William caught sight of the village. It was nestled in a beautiful little
valley just west of the ridge that Komoka had described to him; the one
across which they had just traversed. It became quite obvious that at least
one of the Indians he originally encountered had ran ahead to alert the
village of their arrival, for it seemed the whole village was assembled and
awaiting their entrance.

William spanned the crowd of curious faces in hopes of finding
Komoka but all he saw were unfamiliar stares. Neither did his friend step
out to greet him as he was led through the onlookers to the center of the
village. A whisper of doubt began to rise within him that perhaps this was
not Komoka's village after all. Finally, the Indian leading William stopped
and turned to face an approaching Indian which, by his appearance, gave
William the impression that he was a man of influence in the village,
perhaps a chief. Curiosity gave way to recognition as the man drew
closer—it was Komoka's father! For a brief moment it was as if he had
stepped back in time, for the man's appearance was just like the memory
he had held onto all of these years. Komoka's father greeted William then
invited him to join him in his wigwam so that they could speak privately.

"You must forgive me, sir, but I fear that I have not had the privilege of
learning your given name. Komoka always referred to you as his father,"
William asked as they walked.

"I am called Netawat," he replied. "I am considered a holy man by many of my people for I teach them of the Christian faith; to others I am simply one who is under the spell of the white man," he confessed.

"I take it you do not receive many white visitors in your village," William said as he glanced again at the curious crowd of onlookers.

"You are first in very long time," came the reply as they entered the wigwam and Netawat directed William to a bear rug next to the fire. "Our people have long had peace with the white man, but there are those who would now destroy that peace," he said solemnly. "Some of our squaws have lost husbands to the hatred of these white men. They make war with all Indians regardless of tribe," he continued. He paused and looked into the fire. "The details of your capture were explained to me and of Terrana's desire to kill you. Terrana lost son to white man with who we trade in past," he said as his voice lowered. "The man pretend to be friend and wait for two of our young braves to approach with animal pelts for trade. When they were very close he pull gun from under coat and fire. Another man hide in shelter nearby and fire weapon. Both of our brothers injured but only one return to tell story. Many of my people angry with white man although I know war cause much distrust. I understand that white man has been mistreated by some of our Indian brothers as well," he finished.

William sat quietly for a moment before speaking, "I am truly sorry for the wrong that has been done to your people. It's true that there is much fear among my people because of the increased Indian attacks but there is also some ignorance as well," he continued. "Men are often too quick to judge another by his skin color rather than what is in his heart, I suppose that is commonplace among all races of men. May God help us to see with His eyes and love as He loves," William said sincerely.

Netawat smiled and offered William a morsel of venison from the fire before speaking, "You have grown much since we first meet, and attain great wisdom. I was pleased to see that you still keep the gift Komoka give you that day," he said as he revealed the amulet and handed it to William. "It brought you good fortune today for it save your life."

William took the amulet and held it in his hand for a moment then asked, "When did you last see Komoka?" In his heart an uncertainty and dread had been growing within him since his arrival in the village; he feared that it had something to do with his friend.

Netawat stood to his feet and paced inside the wigwam for several minutes before responding. William's heart began to pound in his chest as he waited anxiously.

Finally, Netawat turned to face William and spoke solemnly, "We receive word this morning that my son captured by Creek Indian chief who calls himself Captain George."

At the name "Captain George" William gasped slightly.

"You know this Indian chief?" Netawat asked, responding to William's obvious reaction to the name.

William explained how Komoka had warned him of Captain George's plans to attack Little Prairie and about the earthquake that very night which had scared them away.

"If it is revenge that is behind my son's capture then it is sure that his life has been taken or will be taken soon, after much suffering," Netawat uttered miserably.

"Have you already sent warriors to search for Komoka?" William asked hesitantly. He did not wish to offend but his curiosity and anger were overpowering his tact.

"We send out small party this afternoon. Instead they find you with amulet," Netawat stated flatly. "A larger party will go tomorrow morning to join those sent to scout," he continued.

William stood to his feet and said boldly, "I will be accompanying them tomorrow morning."

Netawat tried to convince William otherwise, but to no avail. William explained to him his burden to pray for Komoka on the trail back to Cape Girardeau only the week before as well as his confirmation in prayer to seek out his friend. William was convinced that Komoka was still alive because God had plans for him and William to accomplish.

Noticeably touched by William's concern and optimism, Netawat finally agreed to allow William to accompany them the next morning. Afterward, however, Netawat placed his hand on William's shoulder and shared soberly, "I fear that your hope too high, both for Komoka's safety and for his helping you in ministry if he still alive. Although Komoka good man and wise leader he not accept Christian faith as we do," he continued. "He respect you and he not oppose we who follow teachings of Jesus but he not surrender his heart to the Savior," he concluded.

William pondered the events of the day and especially the final words from Komoka's father as he prepared for sleep in the wigwam that he had been taken to after his conversation with Netawat. Doubt toyed relentlessly with his thoughts, but he refused to lose hope. Things were obviously not turning out as he had hoped or planned, but wasn't that somewhat normal in life? Do not the Scriptures say that, *'His ways are higher than our ways and His thoughts than our thoughts'?* William reasoned with himself. He must continue to put his trust in God even when the way seems unclear and dark. He prayed earnestly for his friend before finally succumbing to the weariness of the day and drifting off to sleep.

CHAPTER 32
A MIRACULOUS ESCAPE

Southern Part of Missouri Territory, February 1813

Some forty warriors and one circuit-riding preacher were making their way east as the sun crept over the skyline before them. A solitary eagle soaring overhead seemed to be the only witness to these unusual traveling companions off on what would appear to most as some foolhardy rescue mission. William's horse had been returned to him, so he reached into his saddle bags and, with relief, found that his pistol was still there; he reloaded the weapon as they rode along. He prayed continually as the band pressed forward throughout the morning hours. No one spoke and even in the crisp, cool February air little to no sound was heard from the travelers.

Despite his anxiety over Komoka's plight and the danger of their mission, he couldn't help but feel a sense of awe as he scanned the party of warriors with whom he traveled. In his wildest dreams, he never thought that he, a backwoods Methodist preacher, would be traveling with an Indian war party. With new respect, he regarded their undaunted courage and majestic pride. Tempering this sense of awe, however, was the utter realization that there was an almost undeniable possibility of combat. Would he actually engage in the battle if one ensued? Would he not stand out like a huge target with his pale skin color and darker clothing? Could he, even in good conscience, point his pistol at someone with the intent to kill? He suddenly realized that he could not, at least not unless it was in self-defense. He wrestled with his reaction to whatever may come but felt compelled to forge on ahead. Deep down inside, he held onto the hope that God had a plan, and he didn't want to miss it.

Some of the warriors who had hurried on ahead to scout out the area returned in mid-afternoon and began talking excitedly, but quietly, with Netawat and two other Indian leaders.

When they had finished their conversation, Netawat approached William and quickly relayed to him their message. "The small party of scouts say they come across sign a short distance ahead; they believe it is from Komoka,"

Netawat explained. "Our people have marks that we leave on the earth to alert each other of our presence," he continued. "It is this mark that one brave found but it is possible that Creek warriors see it too. We must hurry," he said as he continued passing the word along.

The band of warriors began running ahead, but still there was little sound. William lagged behind somewhat, keeping his eyes on the warriors in the rear so as not to lose his way. Soon he came up on the group where they had assembled near a stream. William made his way alongside Netawat, who explained that the last sign that was visible ended at this stream and that they had not yet determined where he had exited. The band of Delaware warriors divided their ranks with each group spanning out in opposite directions along the stream. William dismounted and drank from the cold stream water then considered the situation. He was amazed at how the Indian could read sign. He had yet to see anything that would indicate that someone had passed this way. Furthermore, how could they be sure it was Komoka? And perhaps the most striking question was how he could have escaped from his captors if it was, in fact, Komoka?

William looked around nervously as the forest seemed eerily still and vacant. With a hint of fear, he imagined the Creek warriors closing in even now as they too were perhaps following the same sign. Pistol held at the ready, he stood perfectly still as he watched and waited. All of a sudden, from his right he heard a quail call and wondered if it was, in fact, an animal. Within moments, several of the Delaware braves who had followed the stream in the opposite direction began quickly passing William, obviously responding to the quail call. William waited anxiously for several minutes before he finally saw some of his party beginning to filter back in towards him. They were moving very slowly and warily towards him with weapons ready. His concern mounting, he scanned the area around him once again, fully expecting to hear the whoop of the Indians and witness the commencement of a battle at any moment. Seeing nothing, he returned his gaze to the slowly approaching band of Delaware Indians and could see now why they were moving more slowly; there among them was an injured warrior who was being helped along by others. William strained his eyes in an attempt to see if this was indeed his Indian friend. He had a sudden urge to run towards them but knew that they were all still in danger so he resolved simply to wait for them to come to him.

At last they were near enough for William to see that the injured man was, in fact, Komoka. William's heart sank at his appearance for his visage was horribly marred and his near-naked body had been terribly abused. The band stopped in front of William momentarily and William did a quick assessment of his condition. The cold weather had helped to slow the bleeding, but it was obvious that hypothermia was setting in. He grabbed a blanket from off of his horse and wrapped it around Komoka as a couple of the braves lifted the injured man up into the saddle. Although Komoka was in desperate need of medical attention, their immediate concern was putting as much distance as they could between themselves and the Creek Indians. They swiftly began making their way back to the west.

William, leading the horse along, looked back occasionally at his wounded and battered friend. His heart ached inside him as he imagined the horrible torturing Komoka had obviously endured. Strips of the man's skin had been literally torn from his body and it looked as if his face had been struck multiple times for it was badly bruised and swollen. Although weak from the loss of blood, Komoka met William's gaze at one point and attempted a smile. *How had Komoka managed to escape, and how had he gotten here?* These thoughts filled William's mind as they hurriedly made their way back to the Delaware village on the St. Francis River. At times, Komoka swayed in the saddle as he seemed to be going in and out of consciousness. Netawat walked alongside his son and steadied him as well as gave him an occasional drink of water. Soon the sun began to set, but still the party pressed forward.

William breathed a prayer of thanksgiving when the village came into view. The sun had long past set when the party made its way down the ridge and into the group of Indians coming out to meet them. Komoka was quickly taken into his wigwam where several squaws began working with him, cleaning his wounds and administering ointments. William gathered with several of the warriors around a fire where some food was prepared and they all ate as they waited. All were curious as to how their Indian brother had escaped and how he had traveled so far in his condition. Netawat had explained that the Creek village of Captain George was on the other side of the Great River, which was still a good distance beyond where they had found Komoka. Finally, one of the squaws caring for Komoka made her way to Netawat who was sitting beside William near the fire and spoke with him briefly. Without delay, Netawat stood and motioned for William to follow as he began making his way towards Komoka's wigwam.

The strong smell of herbs filled William's nostrils as they entered the wigwam. Once seated next to his friend, he saw that poultices of some combination of herbs and bark had been applied to his many wounds. Netawat touched his son's hand gently and Komoka slowly opened his eyes. His eyes drifted over to William and he once again smiled at his friend as he began to speak. His voice was weak so Netawat encouraged him to rest for now.

"Father, I must speak…there is much to share," came the labored reply. Netawat nodded briefly and waited as Komoka gathered his strength and began.

"Captain George's anger burned strong when I warn white man of planned attack on Little Prairie," Komoka began, speaking weakly. "It was four days ago I travel along the Great River when I meet Creek Warriors. One among them know me and I no can run. They bind my hands and take me across the Great River to village. Captain George take little time in judgment; I to be killed slowly to see if I break and show weakness," Komoka continued with frequent pauses to regain his strength. His eyes closed for a moment and his face grimaced as if reliving in his mind the severe torture he had endured. Opening his eyes, he began again, determined to share something of importance to him despite the physical struggle it required to do so. "I suffer much, but refuse to cry out or even speak," he continued. "My enemies leave me for a time and I begin to call upon the Great Spirit of my forefathers to give me strength to die well. I have listened to my father speak of white man's God and I respect his faith but I always, in some way, feel it is betrayal of our old ways. In this moment I hear a voice…I know not if it real or no. The voice tell me I should call on Jesus and He spare my life…He use me for purpose. For long time I consider this and think of my father and my white friend. Your faith strong and your love for your God very great…this I cannot deny."

Komoka continued, "Finally, I decide to call on Jesus so I lift my voice and ask Him to save me. Soon I hear much excitement in village with many running and yelling. After a time, village become very quiet…no voices or moving for very long time. No warriors coming to beat me. I work with cords that bind me until I free. I look out wigwam where I held prisoner. I see no one so I go through village and feel much fear for everyone gone. Then I see movement in wigwam near other end of village. I find spear that was left behind by Creek Indians and make my way to wigwam. I find another prisoner tied to pole inside. I use end of spear to cut him free then we go to the Great River. He explain that he hear Creek Indian say enemy war party come to attack village. Warriors prepare for battle while women and old ones go to safety. We find canoe and cross the Great River then this Indian make his way south to his village. I walk long time with no food and little water. My injuries make me too weak to continue. I then pray to Jesus that He send my white brother to find me; this will be sign to me that He speak to me. I leave sign on ground to help my Indian brothers find me for I know they look for me. When I see my white brother I know the Christian God real," Komoka said as he lifted his eyes upward. He then looked William in the eye and said resolutely, "I now follow Jesus."

William remained about two weeks with the Delaware people and had the opportunity to open the Word with some of the Christians among them. Komoka healed quickly, despite his many wounds. Before William left, the two were able to discuss at length the burden on William's heart to reach out to the Indian people. Komoka had great interest in the plan and committed to pray for God's direction to that end.

William presented his Indian brother with a new Bible which Komoka accepted thankfully. Komoka's father had learned how to read some and had taught a few of the other men some English. Komoka himself could read a little bit as well, but was eager to learn more. It was little surprise, however, the next day when Komoka presented William with a gift in return—a string of beads with an eagle feather attached to it. Komoka explained that this was a symbol of courage that was often given to an Indian warrior after he had demonstrated bravery in battle. He explained that because William had been willing to face the enemy of his Indian brother then he was worthy of such a gift. William felt like his courage had, in reality, been lacking but he recognized the act as a very gracious gesture on the part of his friend so he humbly accepted the gift.

William then took some time to instruct Komoka concerning the basics of the Good Book. For several hours each day, William explained major themes in Scripture as well as provided Komoka an overview of each book of the Bible.

The thing that surprised his Indian friend the most was that the God of the Bible was not simply the "white man's God" but was, in fact, the God of all creation. "He is the one who created the sun, moon, and stars and is the one who breathed life into man. He is, therefore, the God of all men… regardless of race or color," William explained. Komoka was eager to learn and asked many questions, especially regarding Jesus. He wanted to know more about the One who had spoken to him and answered his prayer so powerfully. Of special interest to him was the story in John chapter four about the woman at the well to whom Jesus offered living water. Having known thirst, both physical and spiritual, Komoka identified with the woman's desire to receive water by which she would never thirst again. He had also experienced that quenching of a deep thirst from which he had secretly suffered for some time. The desire was growing in him to share with his Indian brothers the news of this living water that Jesus gives so freely.

The two friends also discussed the location of different Indian villages in the territory. Komoka traveled much, and was aware of several Delaware and Shawnee villages within two to three days ride of their village on the St. Francis River. They considered the challenges that they would most likely face due to the present political turmoil and pondered possible means to overcome them. Komoka thought it best for him to visit some of the villages first to present the idea and see if they would be open to receiving the minister with a message to deliver. If the feeling was favorable, then an approximate time would be proposed for the visit and Komoka would serve as both guide and translator.

Beyond the great joy William felt in what God had done in the life of his friend, he thoroughly enjoyed the two weeks among the Delaware people. He learned much about their way of life and was in awe at their efficiency in living off of the land. Most of all, he was greatly blessed at how God was truly at work to express his love to all mankind. As William prepared to leave, Komoka made a promise to join his white brother in Cape Girardeau at the first sign of spring. With that, William thanked his gracious hosts and said his goodbyes. Things had not gone exactly as he had planned, he pondered while riding east, but they had proven nonetheless to be divinely orchestrated.

CHAPTER 33
WEDDING DAY

St. Michael, Mid-April 1813

Time had passed quickly since William's short stay with the Delaware Indians. Elder Parker had sat in awe as William relayed the account of Komoka's miraculous escape from the Creek Indian village and his subsequent surrender to the Lord. True to his word, Komoka had arrived at the Travers' cabin on the Whitewater River at the first sign of spring. With some folks still leery of any Indian contact due to the ongoing war, William invited the good elder to meet with him and Komoka at the Travers' cabin rather than having his Indian friend venture into town. The three enjoyed a wonderful season of prayer and Bible study prior to working on details of how and when to begin their outreach. Of course, William's upcoming nuptials were the first order of business and Komoka was determined to accompany the Travers clan as they journeyed to St. Michael for the wedding. William had already made a couple of visits to the Smith cabin on the Castor River and had informed Laura of the events surrounding his trip to find Komoka. She had received William's letter explaining his trip and anxiously awaited news of his safe return. Upon seeing him, she confessed her concern over his plans.

"You know that I greatly admire your service for the Lord," she began sincerely. "I know that there are dangers on the trail and I understand that you will be gone for weeks at a time…these are things that I both understand and accept in becoming a circuit-rider's wife," she continued. "I also believe, like you, that the Indian is made in God's image and needs to hear the gospel message. But what I can't seem to understand is why you feel that now is the time to do this. Not only is there a war going on, but we are to be married in a month!" she proclaimed with a raised voice.

"How can you expect me to be happy about this?" she finished as her eyes filled with tears.

At first it upset William that Laura wasn't excited about his plans or seemingly as happy as others had been about what God had done in Komoka's life. And yet it broke his heart to see Laura crying and so upset. Putting himself in Laura's shoes, he realized how it must have felt to receive a letter such as he had written so close to their wedding. He began to understand, as the two talked, that he would have to be more sensitive to Laura's feelings in his actions and decisions. Taking a wife requires mutual love and respect, and he could no longer just think of his own desires and wants but must consider his wife's as well. Do not the Scriptures say to love your wife as Christ loves the church? The two talked at length about William's passion to reach out to the Indians and prayed together concerning the timing of the plan. Finally, the two decided that William and Komoka would wait until the fall to launch their outreach so that William and Laura could get their home established. Elder Parker agreed that this was for the best; it would also give Komoka adequate opportunity to visit several villages in order to check their openness to ministry. William agreed to maintain his circuit route as well. His hope was that he could foster prayer support for the Indian outreach among some of the families along the route.

The day of the wedding finally arrived, and several families from the St. Michael area had assembled for the grand celebration. With regrets, Elder Parker had informed the couple that he would be unable to join them for the celebration since he would be detained in Indiana for some church business. William was pleased, however, that his friend and fellow circuit rider, Thomas Wright, would be performing the ceremony. Thomas was thrilled at being asked and found great pleasure in reminding William that it was, in part, thanks to him that the couple had met. "You'd still be whining about being a bachelor if I hadn't asked you to help me conduct the camp meetings here in St. Michael," he exclaimed proudly, slapping William on the back.

The womenfolk spent the morning preparing food and talking about their men while the menfolk passed the time swapping yarns. William was thankful for the company and for the distraction, for his nerves were about to get the better of him. He wondered if Laura was as nervous as he was. It was not that he was having second thoughts, but it was just an overwhelming feeling to think that his whole life was about to change. Up until now he only had himself to worry about, but now there would be two mouths to feed—and likely more down the road. And yet, he was content and happy in the knowledge that he would no longer be alone. Sure, he had his ma and pa and there were the many friends he had made along his circuit, but he longed for someone to walk beside him and with whom he could share his most personal thoughts and desires. In his heart, he knew that Laura was the very person God had chosen to be this partner to him.

He was lost in his thoughts when a hand touched his shoulder. He turned to see Komoka smiling at him, "You gonna make it?"

William laughed as he nodded and replied, "You'd think I was gettin' married today wouldn't you? Do Indian braves get this nervous on their wedding day?" Komoka just shrugged as the two rejoined the conversation.

Komoka had joined the Travers family during the trip over to St. Michael a couple days prior. Although William and Laura had taken time to share William's future ministry plans with Harrison and Vera, there was an obvious reservation on Harrison's part to this idea. Upon Komoka's arrival, Harrison became sullen and distant; even on the wedding day he was abnormally quiet. Harrison's faith was young but growing and yet there was obviously a struggle going on in this heart over the presence of an Indian at his daughter's wedding. To his credit, he held his tongue. That, however, could not be said of Reverend Wright. The good reverend liked to talk and began telling stories of past weddings he had performed.

"More than once I have been called upon to perform a Bible wedding weeks after the couple had already considered their marriage contract complete when they promised in the presence of their friends to be husband and wife," Thomas exclaimed. "Of course, this territory is still young and wild and it is not uncommon for us circuit riders to stumble upon places where neither gospel nor law is present," he explained. "There was one place west of here where I wandered a few years back and the bride and groom were each holding a youngin' as I performed the ceremony!" he bellowed. "They told me that they plum tuckered out waitin' on a preacher or the like to come by so they just figured they would make it proper once one finally came along. They paid me with two bushels of turnips for my troubles," he howled as the listeners hooted right along with him.

It was a joyous time of storytelling and laughing as the morning gave way to midday. With the food prepared and the bride primped and ready, the womenfolk announced that the ceremony could begin. The bride and groom took their places next to Reverend Wright while all of their family and friends seated themselves with a few whoops going up for the anticipated union.

As Reverend Wright waxed eloquent about the sanctity of marriage, William stared into Laura's eyes. She looked so lovely, and her sweet personality filled his heart with such joy. Now that he had grown to know and love her, he simply couldn't imagine living life without her. She smiled as if reading his thoughts, tears forming in her eyes. With the Reverend's final amen, William and Laura shared a kiss which immediately kicked off a chorus of whoops and whistles of congratulations for the young couple.

After a time of handshaking and neck hugging, the joyous group made their way over to the wedding feast awaiting them. Among the fixings were wild turkey, roast pig, and fresh baked bread. Before long, William's brother, John, pulled out a fiddle and began to play. Harrison grabbed Vera's arm and whirled her out on the floor and began to dance, much to Laura's delight.

"I haven't seen my parents dance in years!" she exclaimed excitedly. The celebration continued well into the afternoon before some of the folks began to make their way home. William's family had accepted the invitation from the Smith family to stay the night over at their homestead that evening. The cabin that Harrison and some of his neighbors had built for the young couple was ready for its new owners so the remaining family made their way north out of St. Michael a few hours before sundown. Laura was thrilled to show off her decorating prowess, although simple as the furnishings were. Many an hour she had spent over the last several weeks setting up the perfect, cozy abode for her and William's first home. William's mom did not disappoint as she showered Laura with praise over her attention to detail. Of course, there was clear indication of the woman's touch with the doilies and spring flowers, but she had also prepared a corner for William to house his books along with a nice area for him to study.

As the sun began to disappear over the western horizon, the families ate some of the leftovers from their earlier feast and sat along the Castor River watching the dazzling sunset. Although it had been an enjoyable day, fatigue from the day's many activities began to set in. The ladies soon excused themselves and began preparing the bedding for the guests. The men lingered by the river, skipping rocks and chatting a bit. Harrison had opened up more throughout the day and he and Jacob had hit it off quite well. The two shared story after story of experiences they had enjoyed as young boys. As the conversation died down and the sky darkened, Harrison finally stood and wished everyone a good night. William watched curiously as Komoka, who was fully aware of Harrison's avoidance of him since his arrival, stood and made his way over to Harrison.

"I wish apologize to you, on the part of my people, for wrong done to you and family," Komoka shared sincerely. "I hope someday you forgive my people and…" he hesitated for a moment, "know that the God of the white man is also my God."

For a long moment, all that could be heard was the chirping of the crickets and the occasional flop of a fish in the water. It had now become too dark for William to see Harrison's face and he wondered how his father-in-law would react. He had no doubt that Harrison was a new man in Christ, but had he been able to completely turn over to the Lord the many years of anger and bitterness he had harbored over the loss of his son?

William could still make out Harrison's outline in the darkness and watched as Harrison slowly lifted his right hand from his side and offered it to Komoka. An overwhelming sense of relief and joy swept over William as he watched his Indian brother being used greatly by the Almighty to work a healing in the heart of Harrison Smith.

The next day saw the departure of William's family, as well as his Indian friend. Komoka promised to come by in the next couple of months to report on the progress of their ministry venture.

The first week of married life agreed with William as he and his new bride reveled in their new life together. The cool spring mornings found them hand in hand along the Castor River where idle talk and frequent laughter broke the stillness of the picturesque scene. Dreams for the future were discussed along with favorite memories from their childhood. It was a peaceful time—a truly happy moment that they would always hold dear.

In the evenings, William stole away for a time to pray about he and Komoka's ministry plans. One evening in particular, he reminisced about his life thus far and marveled at how the Lord had directed his path. He recalled the booming voice of Reverend McGready and the revival services where he first encountered the power of God. Oh how his heart had burned with the desire to bring the gospel to those scattering across this great new land. Uncle Zeb, of all people, had been the first to make him aware of the circuit-riding preacher and of their courage in braving the elements and dangers of the untamed West to bring the gospel to the lost and dying. How he had fretted those next few years over whether or not the Lord would allow him to become an itinerate minister.

William smiled as he remembered the day he sat across from Elder Parker and Jesse Walker, his heart beating out of his chest in anticipation of their answer as to whether or not he would be admitted as a preacher on trial. How the years had flown! The ministry turned out to be much less glamorous than he had imagined, but rewarding, nonetheless. God was truly faithful and William had grown much, as had the country. This Missouri Territory that he now called home still had many elements of the untamed West, but it was advancing both in number and in progress. Many who had left the more civilized way of life back East with its established churches, schools of higher learning, and organized law enforcement had been unprepared for the stark absence of those elements in the West. Slowly but surely, William could see that chaos was beginning to give way to civility as the Holy Spirit worked in the hearts of the frontiersman. There was still much work to be done, but the fingerprint of the Almighty was evident in the land they called "America."

"Oh God," William prayed, "May Your grace shine down on this great land and Your truth be made known to every man, woman, and child of every race. Amen."

AFTERWORD

Although the Travers and Smith families are fictional, the majority of the remaining names in this story represent actual people who lived and worked in the Midwest during this time period. One example is Jesse Walker, the circuit-riding preacher who mentored William. Reverend Walker actually rode the Cape Girardeau circuit in 1809 and consequently had a significant impact on the early Methodist movement in the young Missouri Territory during his years of service there. Elder Samuel Parker, James McGready, Francis Asbury, William McKendree, Thomas Wright, John Scripps, Barthelimi Cousin, Lorenzo Dow, and Louis Lorimier each contributed in his own way to our country's progress.

Furthermore, many of the events of this story are true as well; most notably the New Madrid earthquake of 1811. Many of the details shared in chapter sixteen are based upon actual firsthand accounts. Finally, the places referred to in our story are also authentic. As a matter of fact, my own childhood years were spent in St. Michael (present day Fredericktown, MO).

One final word concerns the title: Sling Shot Circuit Rider. You will note that rather than the normal spelling of "slingshot," I have written it as two words: "sling shot." The slingshot as we know it today was not invented until later in the 1800s so William was actually using a sling. The play on words is due to the comments made by Mrs. Tidwell in chapter twenty-one of the story, as she was cleverly remarking on William's prowess with the sling.

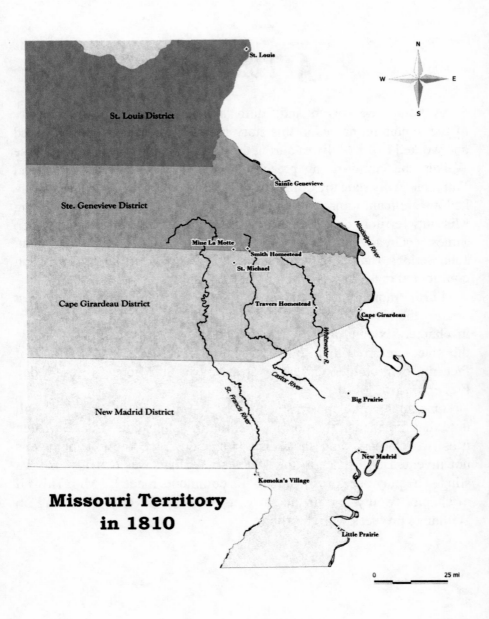

Missouri Territory in 1810

St. Louis District

Ste. Genevieve District

Cape Girardeau District

New Madrid District

St. Louis

Sainte Genevieve

Mine La Motte

Smith Homestead

St. Michael

Travers Homestead

Cape Girardeau

Mississippi River

Whitewater R.

Castor River

St. Francis River

Big Prairie

New Madrid

Komoka's Village

Little Prairie

0   25 mi

N
W   E
S

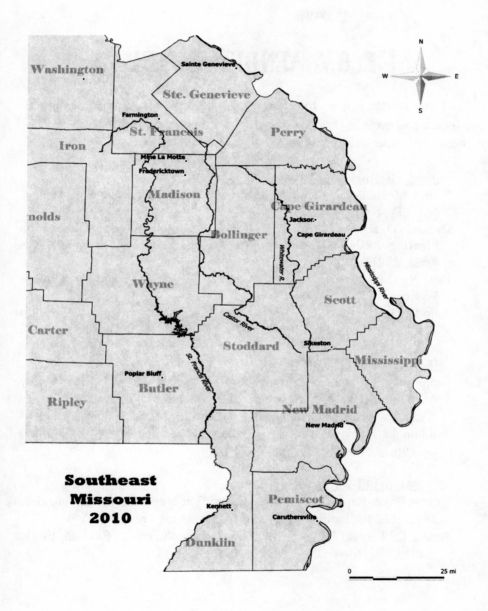

N
W   E
S

Washington

Sainte Genevieve

Ste. Genevieve

Farmington

St. Francis

Perry

Iron

Mine La Motte
Fredericktown

Madison

Cape Girardeau

Jackson

Cape Girardeau

nolds

Bollinger

Whitewater R.

Wayne

Castor River

Scott

Mississippi River

Carter

Stoddard

Sikeston

Mississippi

St. Francis River

Poplar Bluff

Butler

New Madrid

Ripley

New Madrid

**Southeast
Missouri
2010**

Pemiscot

Kennett

Caruthersville

Dunklin

0   25 mi

RECOMMENDED READINGS

I invite the reader to learn more about the history of Southeast Missouri as well as our rich spiritual heritage by checking out some of these recommended resources:

Camp Meetings and Circuit Riders

"Camp Meetings and Circuit Riders," Christian History Magazine, Issue 45 (vo. XIV, No. 1).

Dickson D. Bruce, Jr., And They All Sang Hallelujah: Plain-Folk Camp-Meeting Religion, 1800-1845 (Knoxville: University of Tennessee Press, 1981).

Paul K. Conkin, Cane Ridge: America's Pentecost (Madison: Univ. of Wisconsin Press, 1990).

John O. Gooch, Circuit Riders to Crusades: Essays in Missouri Methodist History (Franklin, TN: Providence House Publishers, 2000).

History of Southeast Missouri

Robert Sidney Douglass, History of Southeast Missouri: A Narrative Account of It's Historical Progress, It's People and It's Principal Interest (Chicago: Lewis Publishing Co., 1912).

William E. Foley, A History of Missouri (V1): 1673–1820 (Columbia: University of Missouri Press, 2000).

New Madrid Earthquake

Norma Hayes Bagnall, On Shaky Ground: The New Madrid Earthquakes of 1811-1812 (Columbia: University of Columbia Press, 1996).

James L. Penick Jr., The New Madrid Earthquakes; Revised Edition (Columbia: University of Missouri Press, 1981).

About the Author

Randy G. Pogue, P.E. has been an ordained minister with the Assemblies of God since 1998. He and his wife, Missy, were appointed Assemblies of God missionaries in 1997 and ministered internationally in France and in Chad, located in North-Central Africa, from 1998 until 2003. Overseas, he was involved in Bible school teaching and church planting. Since 2004, he has been the associate pastor at Arcadia Valley Assembly of God. He is a graduate of the University of Missouri-Rolla (now known as Missouri S&T) with a bachelor's in electrical engineering and has a master of arts in theological studies from the Assemblies of God Theological Seminary in Springfield, Missouri. Along with his pastoral duties at Arcadia Valley Assembly of God, he is also currently employed as an electrical engineer at an electric cooperative in Poplar Bluff, MO. His wife, Missy, is a registered nurse and has used her skills on the mission field as well as here at home in the United States. They have three children, Elizabeth, Samantha, and Will.

More Titles by 5 Fold Media

45 Minutes
by Kristen Young
$15.00
ISBN: 978-1-936578-10-8

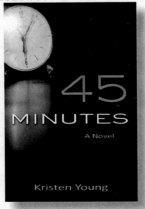

45 Minutes by Kristen Young is the undeniable journey of Anthony Michaels' life, which is oddly typical until he faces an encounter with eternity. Readers will relate to the characters as they read about painful life lessons, true forgiveness, answered prayers and the love of God that can change any situation.

45 Minutes was written with the purpose of helping readers see the unfailing love of God. The author hopes that this book will draw people into a relationship with their Savior as they see themselves through the eyes of the characters.

Beyond the Moment
by Jean Kashella
$17.00
ISBN: 978-1-936578-08-5

Beyond the Moment by Jean Hudak-Kashella is a fiction story revealing simple spiritual truths. When one man's compassion for teens collides with real-life obstacles, a series of miraculous events ensue. And, when he finds romance and meets his father for the first time, his vulnerability becomes evident.

Beyond the Moment is a story of love, loss, and how God's grace bridges the gap. The author uses a unique style of descriptive writing that captivates the reader as they become inspired in simple spiritual truths.

Visit www.5foldmedia.com to sign up for 5 Fold Media's FREE email update. You will get notices of our new releases, sales, and special events such as book signings and media conferences.

5 Fold Media, LLC is a Christ-centered media company. Our desire is to produce lasting fruit in writing, music, art, and creative gifts.

"To Establish and Reveal"
For more information visit:
www.5foldmedia.com

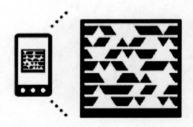

Use your mobile device to scan the tag above and visit our website.
Get the free app: http://gettag.mobi

CPSIA information can be obtained at www.ICGtesting.com
Printed in the USA
LVOW051402160912

298989LV00007B/101/P